CHASING MURDER

A.M. Holloway

Your Book Company

eBook ISBN: 9781956648171

Paper ISBN: 9781956648188

Library of Congress Control Number: 2022917237

Chapter 1

Birds sat on tree branches outside my window, singing their favorite song while I sat in the lone recliner, trying to determine how I would survive this life without my husband. Everyone said every day would get easier. So, why hasn't it?

When Captain Swank showed up on my doorstep, I knew Casper was gone without him uttering a word. My husband, Casper, loved police work. He swore he'd never leave the job until they forced him to retire. Casper was a detective in the major case squad. They investigated the worst of the worst. Someone ambushed Casper and his partner on a downtown street, and both died at the scene.

My breath comes in short bursts as I see Captain Swank at the door. Every time I close my eyes, I see him and hear him say, "I'm sorry, Celeste." Then everything turned dark, and I awoke alone in a hospital bed because there was no one to call. My room was dark and filled with flowers. Finally, a nurse stopped in to check on me, sharing that I'd missed twenty-four hours of my life.

When they let me leave the hospital, Captain Swank drove me home. He chatted about the weather. Then he asked if I would consider staying at a friend's cabin in the northern Colorado mountains. "It might be good for you, Celeste. You know until you can get your feet under you." He glanced at me, but I stared straight ahead.

"I'll think about it." Then he dropped me off at my house because I wanted to enter it alone. I stood at the door for a minute, telling myself I could do this. But, when I entered the house, I hit my knees, yelling, "why me?"

I never got my answer, but I knew I couldn't stay on the floor forever, so I pushed myself to move forward. The first thing I did was check my messages on my cell phone. I couldn't listen to the callers expressing their sadness, so I deleted those. But when the medical examiner's office left a message. I listened to it because I needed instructions on how to bury Casper.

After I set the appointment with the funeral home, I packed Casper's things. Unfortunately, I couldn't take the time to revisit the memories of when he bought certain items. Instead, I just threw everything in boxes.

Then I took the captain up on his offer of staying in a mountain cabin. This time of year would be excellent if the snow stayed away. I sat in Casper's recliner, breathing in his smell with plans in the works. Would I ever accept his death? It was too early to know that answer.

Three weeks after the funeral, I drove to a remote cabin in the White River National Forest, west of

Denver. Since we moved to Colorado, I'd never been to the northern mountains. They were a sight to behold. We have mountains in Colorado Springs, but nothing like these.

As I settled in, I realized how quaint the cabin was as it's nestled at the base of a mountain. This was postcard perfect. The captain provided me with a map of the area in case I wanted to wander around. I enjoyed a good hike, so that sounded fun until I realized Casper wasn't with me.

Since the sun began drifting below the horizon, I opted to stay inside. Then, when I hiked tomorrow, it would be in the daytime with bright sunshine and no chance of rain.

The following day, I toyed with the idea of hiking alone in an unfamiliar area. But finally, I tried a short hike, not venturing too far away. The scenery was breathtaking. All forms of wildlife posed for pictures on my first hike. By the time I returned to the cabin, I had smiled for the first time since Casper's death.

My cell phone beeped with texts and voicemails, and I still couldn't bring myself to answer them yet. I had taken a six-month leave of absence from my work as a nurse, so I had no reason to answer them. Even though I knew I would in time. I kept a list of every caller and text so I didn't forget anyone.

I slept through the night for the first time since Casper died. When I rolled over and checked my phone, the time shocked me. Then I glanced around, making sure I was still in the cabin. I'd need to check in with Captain Swank today since I'd promised to call him once a week. He worked it out for me to stay here for a month, thinking that would be long enough.

Over the next several days, I ventured out a little further each day. And each day, I found something new and exciting. My phone held more pictures than ever, and I couldn't wait to load them into my laptop and make a memory book. Something that I can keep forever.

On one of my hikes, I found another cabin that sat next to a clearing. The grass blew with the wind, creating a mesmerizing sight. I sat on a tree stump and watched for a while until my eyes grew tired. I promised myself I'd revisit this spot before I left for home.

My last week at the cabin was somber. While I enjoyed my time away, I needed to return to my life, whatever that looked like without Casper. I'd have to make it my own.

The middle of the week seemed like the perfect time to revisit the field, giving it one more look and another set of photos. So, I loaded my small backpack with bottled water and a few granola bars, and off I went. I held a walking stick with one hand to help keep me upright while the other held my phone. I snapped photos as I walked because I didn't want to miss anything.

As I crested the rise in the field, I thought I heard voices. I glanced behind me, focusing on the cabin, but it stood dark like before. When I lifted my phone to take a picture, I heard, "get her."

My eyes scoured the field for the source of the words, then a gunshot echoed and a man ran at me from a hundred yards away.

I turned to run, but my mind wouldn't work. During my marriage, Casper taught me how to handle certain situations. This was one of them. Casper's voice told me to run but not return to the cabin. So, I ran in the opposite direction. Since I had no clear direction, the path mattered to no one.

As I sprinted away, I dropped my phone in my backpack. Then I realized I wore jeans, a long sleeve t-shirt, and boots. My coat lay across the bed in the cabin. How long could I survive in the Colorado Mountains dressed like this?

The thought brought shivers, but I couldn't dwell on it because I heard heavy footsteps behind me. So, I pushed my body harder than I'd ever done before. I started zigzagging as I ran, hoping I would find another cabin or a person. After a mile, I was still alone. Then I chastised myself for not bringing my handgun. Casper taught me how to shoot and reminded me it's better to have it on me and not need it than the other way around.

As I ran, I noticed a slight rise in the ground as I followed it along its base. I slowed, wondering if the man was still behind me. When I heard nothing, I stopped. Then my heart rate increased when I found an opening in the small hill. I tried to cover my tracks the best I could, then crawled inside using my phone's flashlight.

After I checked for bears, I leaned against the wall, praying the man didn't find me. A few minutes later, I heard movement, and there were two men this time. "Where could she have gone?" one man said.

Then the other one, "do you think she saw us?"

"How do I know?" the first guy barked.

Then footsteps beat the ground as they raced away, still searching for me. I smiled again, thinking I was safe for the time being. The next thing I remembered was how cold it was in the cave. I had dosed off after the two men left. Now nighttime had fallen, and so had the temperature.

I crept to the cave's entrance, peeking outside. The forest was pitch black until a sliver of moonlight cut through the treetops. Once I crawled out, I stood, shaking the dirt from my clothes. Then I began a slow trek, heading away from the men. Captain

Swank's map showed a small town south of my cabin, but I had run the opposite way.

Five hundred yards from the cave, I heard the same voices. I froze as they grew closer. Since I couldn't see them, I ducked behind a low bush, almost crawling inside. Will these guys ever give it up? I can't run around the mountain forever with only one bottle of water and half of a granola bar.

When I stood from my hiding place, I groaned as a raindrop slid down my face. Looking to the heavens, I knew I was in trouble. Clouds now covered the moon. Unfortunately, those clouds weren't only rain clouds, but they held buckets of snow. That made me nervous because, for the first time since the gunshot, I was unsure if I'd make it off this mountain alive.

Without the moon, walking turned treacherous. Then, with the added moisture, the ground turned slick. My upper body was icy, so I jogged in place, trying to get my blood circulating, hoping I would warm up. After several minutes, I walked a little further until I ended at the mountain's edge. If I hadn't studied my surroundings, I could have easily walked off into the abyss with no one finding me.

I backed away from the edge, walking around the gorge until I found another path. I stopped long enough to glimpse my map. Unfortunately, Captain Swank didn't point out the gorge. So, he probably thought I'd never walked this far. Then I chastised myself for not going back for my jacket. But Casper always said that when you run, never return to where you started. So, I didn't. But I sure could use a coat.

I traversed along the gorge's side, listening for anything that sounded like footsteps. My hike was slow because of the downward pull and slick ground. After I had walked for a while, I was too tired to figure out how far I'd come. I found a small outcropping of rocks and slid my body underneath for some protection from the weather.

One sip of water, and I laid back on the rocks. When I awoke, the sun had risen behind the clouds, but the temperature failed to follow. Forgoing water and food, I prepared myself for another hike. After all this walking, I'm grateful Casper pushed me to exercise. I was athletic in high school, but my exercise days with a demanding job dwindled as I got older.

Gym dates were the fun dates when we exercised together. It made the time fly instead of feeling like it dragged on as you jumped from one exercise to another. Casper taught me to stretch before any rigorous activity. So, after stretching, I trudged forward.

I thought I heard a noise, but it sounded strange, not like voices, but mechanical. Since I didn't hear it again, I walked further. Then, as I held onto a tree for support, I heard it again. It was a helicopter flying overhead. My heart rate increased when I thought they would rescue me, but then my mind took over, telling me it might be the guys chasing me. So, how could I spot the difference from that distance?

Without another option, I had to chance it. I was almost out of water and food. With my hands above my head, I screamed and waved frantically at the helicopter. I thought they saw me for a second, but they flew away. As they passed overhead, someone hung out the side of the copter, looking through binoculars.

Something niggled at me, but I ignored it. Instead, I raced down the mountain, trying to find a visible spot for them to see me. Unfortunately, the rain came down in a steady cadence, and I knew that made it more difficult for them to spot me.

The only way to prove my location was by screaming and waving my arms because I had no flare. Matches would've created smoke, but everything was so damp, I didn't think they would start a fire.

A few hundred yards later, I found a small area where I could see the sky without tree branches. When the helicopter returned, I began screaming and waving my arms before I could see. The copter hovered in place for a few seconds before the first gunshot sounded. It created such an echo that I flinched before I felt the sting.

It registered when a guy fired a rifle, sending the bullet close to my shoulder. The men in the helicopter were out to catch me. I wanted to scream for other reasons than to be found. These men were relentless in their pursuit to the point of being annoying. Now, instead of being scared, I was angry.

I sprinted away from the area with as much speed as my wounded leg would allow. Somehow, I needed separation from these guys because blood seeped into my boot as I ran. It would need medical attention, and that takes time.

Looking at my surroundings, I wondered how far I was from the cave. That would be the perfect cover, but I didn't know how to find it. So, I threw that idea away and searched for another. Then my heart sank as the largest snowflake in history passed before my eyes heading to the ground.

My inner self struggled to maintain a positive outlook as every turn brought more obstacles. By the time I slowed, I was hobbling because my leg hurt every time I set it on the ground. I worked on finding a reason for the pain. My leg didn't appear broken, so it was muscle issue.

Finally, I gave in to the pain, so I wrestled myself under a large bush. It wasn't completely dry underneath, but it gave me the room I needed. I plucked my phone from my bag when I noticed the dark screen. Now, I had no phone and no flashlight.

Then I remembered Captain Swank. He should be worried since I didn't check in with him. Maybe he's notified law enforcement, and someone is scouring the area for me. But I couldn't count on it. Since I've rationed my supplies, I only have enough for another day. Then, I had no clue what to do from there.

I gently raised my pant leg, but it wouldn't lift more than two inches. So, I ran my hand over the area, finding the culprit. The bullet must have struck a rock, sending a fragment through my pants leg into my leg. It felt like my leg was on fire. I had no tweezers, but I carried gauze and band-aids. My fingertips grazed the tip of the rock fragment, and I winced when it moved. Grasping both sides of the rock, I pulled it out. Blood spurted from the hole. I let it bleed for a moment, cleaned the wound, then placed a butterfly bandage on it, covering it with gauze since the wound was too large for a band-aid.

Once I secured the bandage, I realized how groggy I had become. My body told me to rest between the blood loss and the race to safety. I curled up in a fetal position, trying to stay warm, and fell into a dream-filled sleep. A faceless man chased me down the hallways of a large building. He would pop out from behind a picture, a door, and a desk. It felt like I ran forever. Then the helicopter flew over. I dared not move for fear of being seen.

I waited for what felt like an hour, and the helicopter never reappeared. So, I began my trek and promised myself I'd make it to a town or another cabin this time. I heard no footsteps or helicopters flying overhead this time, and I wondered why. Is the weather changing, and I'm unaware, or did the men give up thinking I wouldn't make it out alive? Well, I'd prove them wrong if that was the last thing I did.

My leg wouldn't allow me to walk down the mountain because the pain was too great. Also, I didn't want it to bleed again. I needed my strength. So, I walked parallel to the mountain's bottom, thinking I would find a cabin before I made it to town. After several miles, the sky grew darker. I didn't know what to expect, snow or rain, but either would hamper my progress.

Then I rounded a corner and stared at a small one-room cabin. My pulse ticked upward at the thought of heat, but it dwindled when I hobbled up the steps, finding the door locked. I wasn't one to break inside. Instead, I found the crawl space. It wasn't large, but it would keep me out of the weather.

Once I closed the door behind me, I shimmied to the far side. So, if someone opened the door, the outside light wouldn't give my location away. Then I collapsed. I could go no further until I rested.

When I awoke, it was freezing inside this crawl space. I returned to the door and tried to push it outward, but it wouldn't move. Something or someone prevented the door from opening.

I worked through my thoughts, trying to clear my mind. While I heard nothing overnight, I might have slept so hard that nothing would have woken me. I turned my body, so my feet were against the door, then pushed with all my might. Then I remembered my leg wound. All I needed was for it to bleed again.

The door moved, and I gasped at the amount of snow that poured into the crawl space. How was I supposed to hike through a foot of snow with my injured leg? I inhaled, preparing myself for the outside.

I crawled out of the tight space on all fours, sinking in the snow that lay next to the cabin. When I stood, I surveyed my surroundings. Things didn't look so bad. Snow had fallen, but the wind had pushed it against the cabin, leaving some bare patches on the ground. Since I saw or heard no one, I began another trek.

My leg slowed me, but I kept pushing. Snow drifts prevented me from walking somewhat of a straight line, so I had to concentrate on staying on the path while monitoring my surroundings. The clouds would break for a minute. Then they moved back in place, overtaking the sun.

My body was numb to the temperature, and my hunger pains were gone. Since I was out of the water, I stopped and filled my water bottle with snow. If only I'd paid attention to Casper when he talked about what to eat in the forest.

The more I thought about food, the hungrier I became. So I thought about what I'd do if I saw the men again. As I walked, I glanced around for hiding places because I liked to have a plan.

Then I felt it. Blood seeped down my leg into my boot. How was I ever going to stop it? I had to use my leg to walk, and without crutches, I had no option. I used the last of my bandages as I worked to staunch the blood flow. Then I wondered if the rock fragment pierced a vein. If it did, I might not make it to town, anyway.

It had been hours since I left the crawlspace, and I had heard nothing on my walk. By Swank's map, I should be close to town. So, why haven't I seen anyone? Trailheads start in town, leading to cabins and camping sites, but I've seen nothing like that.

I pushed myself to keep moving because if I didn't, I'd freeze or starve to death, unsure which would win the battle. Then more light began filtering through the treetops, and my hope surged with eagerness to see what sat in the opening.

When I rounded the corner of a slight rise, I breathed a sigh of relief. I did it! A truck stop sat a hundred yards away. But I stopped when I got to the wood's edge for fear of being in the open. I watched people come and go from the truck stop for a few minutes. But eventually, food and warmth urged me to enter the shop.

I pushed through the door to the shop and walked into the restroom so I could clean my face. The person staring back at me was unfamiliar. My eyes were dark, dirt caked my face, and my hair had debris sticking out.

After washing my face and scrubbing my hands, I worked to free the debris from my hair. That proved more challenging than I thought since I had no brush or comb. Once I felt presentable, I returned to the shop. At least I was smart enough to carry my wallet in my bag, so I had money to eat.

I ordered coffee and a full breakfast. My body took the nourishment in stride, but I found I had been without food for so long that it caused me to eat slowly. This gave me time to watch people. I was curious to see if the men chasing me were here.

My server approached with a concerned expression. "Excuse me, are you okay?"

"I've had a rough few days. I need to charge my phone so that I can call the police. Can you help me?" I muttered.

"Sure, I can, but you must look at your leg. It looks like you're bleeding." The server pointed to my leg like I didn't know where it was.

When I glanced down, I grimaced. "Great." I stammered as I reached for a wad of napkins. Sliding my leg under the table so no one would see it, I pressed the napkins to my leg, hoping to slow the blood flow.

The server was gone when I straightened up in the booth. Even with my leg bleeding, I couldn't leave this food. So, I applied pressure to my wound and shoveled the remaining food into my mouth. When I'd finished, I waved my hand to my server so I could get my check. She approached quickly, "can you give me my check? I need to see about this leg."

"Let me help you. Wait here just a moment." She rushed off, returning with a check that said paid on it.

"You don't need to do that. I have money to pay for my food."

She shook her head, "you might have the money, but by the looks of your leg, you've got bigger problems than paying for your meal. Let's get you into the restroom, and then we'll work on your leg. Besides, Blaine is on his way."

"Blaine?" I asked with a concerned tone.

"Yes, Detective Blaine Crosby. He comes in here all the time. You'll like him. He'll help you get your situation corrected." The lady reached over and helped me stand. But when I stood upright, I faltered as my blood pressure plummeted. I'd have hit the floor if I hadn't been leaning on the lady.

"Sorry," I muttered. Then I asked, "what's your name?"

"Hazel." She said, then she asked, "do you know those men?" Hazel pointed off to the side at two men staring at them.

It scared me to look, but I knew I needed to. When I did, I froze. Those were the two men following me. I couldn't put Hazel in danger, so I said, "you need to return to work. I can't have you getting hurt because of me. How long until Blaine gets her?"

"I'm not sure. He didn't tell me where he was when I called him."

Hazel looked around then suggested, "go to the bathroom, and while you work on your leg, charge your phone." She passed me a phone charger. I blessed her as I hobbled off.

There was no chair or sofa in the ladies' room, so I propped myself on the wall with my leg hoisted over the sink. This time, I was unsure if I could stop the bleeding. Just as I was about to give up, the door opened, and in walked Hazel.

"Here. Use these. It might help with the pressure."

"How did you know?" I met her eyes as she shared her idea.

"I could tell you're comfortable in the woods, but you're from the city. Something bad happened to you, and you fought to get here. I figured it was a man since they're good for stuff like this. Are those two men out there the ones chasing you?" Hazel asked in a terse tone.

I nodded, then added, "please get no more involved than what you've already done. I couldn't handle it if they hurt you because of me." Then my phone messages started dinging.

We chuckled when the sound finally stopped. "What's your name?" she asked me.

"Celeste Kerne. I've been staying at a cabin in the mountains when I saw something I shouldn't have, and I've been on the run for days. This wound is from a bullet's ricochet."

"Well, Celeste. It's nice to meet you. Even under these circumstances. I'll keep the guys away from the door, and then I'll let Blaine know where you are when he arrives."

I thanked Hazel as I scrolled through my messages. Captain Swank had many calls and texts, getting more worried with every note. I dialed him first. He answered on the first ring, and my eyes filled with tears at hearing his voice.

Captain Swank asked for details and told me to stay put. When I shared about Detective Crosby, he told me to call back when I met him, and he would call Blaine's captain. My nerves settled until someone knocked on the door, then I froze. I refused to answer, since I had no idea who was on the other side.

The pounding grew in intensity. Then I heard someone ask the knockers if they needed help. This caused the pounding to stop. So, after a few moments, I cracked the door open, peering outside. No one stood at the door, so I walked in the opposite direction, sliding out the side door and into the woods. When Hazel returns searching for me, she'll find my cell phone number on a mirror, written in my blood.

Chapter 2

I thought leaving was a good idea, but the further I made it from the store, the weaker I became. My vision blurred, and my head hurt. Being a nurse, I knew the signs. I'd be unconscious in minutes and needed a place to hide. But somewhere, Hazel could find me.

The next thing I remembered was hearing muffled voices. I lifted my eyelids ever so slightly, trying to figure out what was happening. Then I heard Hazel's voice, "she's waking. Come on, Celeste. Wake up. Detective Crosby is here, and you're safe."

I couldn't seem to focus on Hazel, but another face appeared behind her. Then I got scared until she told me to calm down. She introduced me to Detective Blaine Crosby, but I couldn't speak. Instead, he said, "Celeste lay still. An ambulance is en route to take you to the hospital."

His voice was pleasant and authoritative, so I gave in, trusting that this guy knew what he was doing.

I dared not move when I awoke because my surroundings were unfamiliar and who sat beside me was a mystery. I remember speaking with Captain Swank, but how long ago was that? Focus returned to my eyes, and I noticed IVs attached to my arm, but I couldn't read what type of medication flowed through the tubes from where I lay.

I coughed as I tried to swallow, and two people jumped up from their chairs. Hazel approached first. "Welcome back, Celeste. You gave us a scare."

"Thank you." I squeaked out. While squeezing her hand, I glanced at the guy standing behind her.

"Celeste, this is Detective Blaine Crosby. We found you in the woods. Good idea leaving your phone number on the mirror." I nodded and tried to smile, but I failed miserably.

"Hi, Celeste. I'm staying here with you until we find those guys. You rest, then we'll talk."

I glanced at Hazel, and she nodded, knowing I'd be okay with Blaine. Then I closed my eyes. Dreams filled my mind as I revisited the last few days. I saw Casper's face as he grinned. Then he told me I was a good girl, and I learned well. Before he faded, he told me to accept my new life.

Somehow, Blaine knew I struggled in my sleep because he was rubbing my arm when I woke. I glanced down at his head as he laid it on the bed's side. "I'm awake," muttering through a dry mouth.

"You must have had some dream. I'm glad you're awake. Are you ready for ice chips? That's all you can have right now."

I nodded as I felt a tear fall to the pillow. Blaine said when he faced me again, "I hope I didn't upset you." His thumb caught the second tear before it left my face. Our eyes met, then he said, "there's no need for tears. You're in capable hands. I promise."

Blaine stood by my bedside, feeding me one ice chip at a time until I couldn't eat anymore. "I need to call Captain Swank because I'm sure he's worried." I stammered.

"No need. We've been in constant contact since I found you. When you notified him of your predicament, he called my captain. I was already on my way to the truck stop when my captain called me. Hazel just had a head start." He grinned as he explained what had transpired.

I stared at Blaine, taking it all in. Dark hair with a hint of gray at the temples paired with pale blue eyes was a great combination. Then he caught me staring.

"Something wrong, Celeste?"

I gathered myself, then said, "no, not really. Just grateful to be here. I'm unsure if I would have survived if not for Hazel." As I tried to move in the bed, a sharp pain radiated from my leg to my heart. "Whoa. What happened to my leg?"

Blaine hesitated but gave me the details. The doctors found a piece of rock embedded in my leg, piercing a vein. I would've never stopped the blood flow in the woods. Blaine described the surgery that took hours to repair my vein. He ended his spiel by stating they expected me to make a full recovery, but it would be a few weeks before I could use my leg.

I grimaced, then added, "I'm a nurse. How am I supposed to work if I can't walk?"

"I can't answer that, but you will walk again. Do you feel like talking about the two guys that chased you?" Blaine inquired.

"Sure. I can do better than that. Their pictures are on my phone." I glanced around for my things, but I didn't see them. "Do you know where my backpack is?"

Blaine stood and reached into the small closet. He handed my backpack to me, and it felt good to touch something Casper had once held. I rummaged to the bottom, coming out with my phone.

It was dead again. "It's dead. I don't have a charger because I left it in the cabin where I was staying." I explained, hoping he wouldn't ask me questions about that.

But that didn't work. "Why were you staying alone in the mountains?"

Pausing before I answered, I told him the truth. "My husband died, and I went to work through my grief.

While I was hiking, I spotted the men who shot someone, and then the chase began."

"Celeste, I'm so sorry to hear about your husband. If I had known, I wouldn't have asked."

"I understand. My husband was a detective, like you. He and his partner were ambushed." When I made the statement, I waited for the tears. None came. I was proud of that baby step, anyway.

Blaine's eyes turned dark as he absorbed my statement. He said nothing as he rubbed his neck. Then he nodded his head. "It makes sense now. Captain Swank said you were fragile. I took it as physical, not in the grief sense." Then he smiled as he added, "you're definitely not fragile physically. I don't know of another woman who could have survived what you did alone."

We stared at each other. Then I thought about how lucky I was to meet Hazel and Blaine. But what happens next? As I lay there pondering my next steps, I dozed.

Then a loud noise jarred me from my sleep. I heard yelling and metal things crashing to the floor. When I tried to move, I couldn't. I waited for the melee to end, then I heard a gunshot.

I couldn't lay in bed any longer. What happened, and where is Blaine?

Swinging my legs off the bed was the most painful thing I can remember. Then I had to maneuver the IV stand, too. People were yelling and running around. I needed to know if Blaine was okay.

The yelling had ceased when I made it to the door. Blaine stood over a guy lying on the floor. He spoke to someone on the phone, giving a description. Then a nurse pointed toward me. He turned and ran to my side. He wrapped his arms around me, and I melted. Blaine was a head taller, and I felt safe until I glimpsed the floor.

He ended his call. "What are you doing out of bed? You're not supposed to be using your leg."

"With all this ruckus, you expected me to stay in bed." I peered up at him, then at the guy on the floor. The attendants rolled him on his side, slid a board underneath him, then lifted him to a gurney. That's when I saw the guy wearing scrubs.

"What happened, Blaine? Tell me the truth." I gazed at him, daring him to tell a lie.

He told me that two guys wearing all black and dark sunglasses entered the lobby. The lady at the desk warned him of their presence. They arrived before Blaine was ready, and as they approached my room, a nurse tried to intervene, but they shot him in the shoulder. Blaine exited my room with his gun drawn, but the two men escaped down the stairwell before being stopped.

"Swell. They know I'm here. I should call Captain Swank and have him pick me up."

Blaine struggled with that idea. "I'd rather you stayed with me."

His comment shocked me. I really didn't have a reply other than, "with you?"

"Those men potentially murdered someone. It happened in my town. You're the only witness. They won't quit chasing you. Let me finish it." Blaine's eyes pleaded with me. So who was I to argue?

"Can I think about it?"

He grinned, but he knew he had me. So instead of letting me walk back to bed, he scooped me up in his arms, placing me gently on the bed. "I'll be right back. I need a word with my captain and the hospital administrator." Blaine said.

Then I asked, "can you leave your backup gun with me? I can shoot."

Blaine's eyes grew wide, and then he broke into a grin as he reached for his ankle holster. He handed me his backup weapon butt first.

I placed it in the grip of my hand. "Snub nose 38 S&W. Nice. Now, do your thing. I'm ready for whatever happens until you return."

He offered no words, just a grin. Then I watched him leave. I had no idea what plans he had in mind, but these guys won't stop until I'm dead. So, it makes me wonder who they killed and why. Did I stumble into something much larger than I first suspected?

Something told me to go back to the scene. Let Blaine inspect it, and maybe he could find evidence tying these guys to the murder. Then my phone beeped. Something I haven't heard in a while.

Hazel texted for an update. My heart swelled when I saw her name pop up on my screen. I replied with the short version of the attack. She wanted to sit with me, and I explained Blaine had a plan and that I'd let her know once I knew his plan.

Then Swank called. I was unsure if I should answer, but I wanted to hear his voice. Captain Swank let out a tremendous sigh when he heard my voice. I did the same. He asked if he could come to get me, but he understood when I explained about the crime scene being here and Blaine's request. Then he shocked me when he described Blaine's record of cases solved. It impressed me more than I cared to acknowledge. We agreed to keep in touch.

A group stood outside my door talking, but I couldn't understand their words. So I stayed ready with the gun covered by sheets. There was no way I would give in to sleep until someone was with me.

Blaine entered my room in a rush. "We're moving you to a secure room at the end of the hall. No one enters without an ID and password. You'll have a guard if I can't be here."

"If the room is secure, I'll be fine. But I'd like you to take me back to my cabin and the crime scene. You should see it."

"Unfortunately, you can't go anywhere until the doctor releases you, and you still have a few more days. It seems rocks carry germs, and they're treating you for infection." He pointed to the IV holding the infection medication.

"As soon as they let me walk, I'm ready. I can't lay here forever." I grimaced as I tried to move my leg. Then I stared at it because I couldn't explain why it didn't feel better. I've been in this bed for days, and it hurts just as much as it did when I got here.

"What's wrong, Celeste? Do I need to get a nurse?" Blaine asked as he walked closer to the bed.

"No. I was thinking about my leg and wondering why it didn't feel better. It's time I discuss my injury with the doctor. They're not telling us everything." Blaine was taken aback by my statement, and he tried to soften his response.

"Celeste, you had surgery. You have stitches inside and outside your leg. Of course, it's going to hurt. Every step will pull those stitches and if one rips."

I raised my hand, stopping him in mid-sentence. "I know that I'd be right back where I started. It's frustrating when I can't do things for myself."

"In time, Celeste, in time. I have a meeting with the hospital administrator and security team leader. I'll be away for a few hours as soon as your guard arrives, but I'll be back."

I nodded because I was unsure how I felt about someone else watching my back. Then another guy knocked on my door. He was Blaine's age, shorter but stocky. Blaine thanked him for showing up so quickly.

The new guy said, "So this is Celeste. Nice to meet you." He shook my hand and saw the weapon under the sheet. He glanced back at Blaine.

"Celeste, this is Detective Carter Eden. He's my partner and the best in the business." Blaine said.

"Wow, Detective Crosby, you're throwing it on thick," Carter said with a wink.

I got lucky again. Blaine walked to my bedside, slipped his hand under the sheet, and took his gun. Then he whispered, "you don't need this anymore. He has two." He winked as he left.

Carter sat beside me in Blaine's chair, but somehow it worked. They favored mannerisms and looks. I'd get the backstory at some point, but right now, I was sleepy.

I shifted in bed and grimaced as the pain shot up my left side. Then, once I settled, I fell into a dreamless sleep. There were no faces, no chases, and Casper didn't speak to me.

When I awoke, Carter sat in the same chair but held a coffee cup this time. I waited for him to speak. "How'd you sleep?"

"The best sleep in a while. Thanks for guarding me, Carter. You all have been the best." I meant every word I said, and he knew it.

A new nurse stopped at the door, provided Carter with her ID, then whispered the password into his ear. He slid from the doorway, allowing the nurse access. When she approached the bed, she said, "Celeste, you sure have cute bodyguards." I looked at Carter, then laughed. Something I haven't done in days.

I asked to see my doctor, and the nurse advised me he'll be around later in the day. After she checked my vitals, I asked for the results. She stared at me, then I explained, "I'm an RN back home in Colorado Springs."

"Really? That's great. If you need a job, let us know. We're short on folks now." Then the nurse recited my vitals, which pleased me to hear them. Now, my concern was my leg.

"So, what can you tell me about my leg?" I didn't elaborate. Instead, I waited for her to answer.

"You spent three hours in surgery for the surgeon to reattach several veins and one artery. They removed rock fragments as they went. They're 80% certain you won't need another surgery, but it's hard to be 100% when they pull rock chips from your muscles. You'll need physical therapy because of the intensity of the surgery, but you're in great physical shape, so I see no problem with that. It's the time needed to heal."

"Thank you for your information. I feel better knowing what I face." As she finished entering my data into her computer, Blaine returned sooner than I expected.

"I'm here for the move. Then I need to step away again. Everything okay, Eden?"

"Yes. Celeste took a good nap. Then this lovely nurse stopped by. So, I'd say everything is perfect." Carter smiled as his eyes sparkled.

I glanced at the nurse as she blushed. That was cute. I read her name tag in case Carter wanted it later. The tag had Alena Hundy printed on it.

Alena's radio beeped, and she replied she was in my room, and then the instructions were for her to assist in my move. So she helped gather my things and rolled me down the hallway to a corner room.

This room had more windows on each side and a locking door. She reattached the IV to another monitor and removed the old one, leaving Carter and me alone. He plopped down into the chair and sighed. "This chair is much better." He grinned, trying to make light of the circumstances.

I laid my head back because I wondered what Blaine was doing. He didn't know where the crime scene was because I hadn't shared that with anyone. Then I remembered the pictures. "Detective Eden, I forgot to give the pictures to Blaine."

"You can call me Carter. What pictures?"

"I snapped photos of the two men that I saw kill someone. Unfortunately, my phone was dead, so I haven't shown Blaine. But he needs to see it." I answered in an anxious tone.

"It's okay. Let me see your phone, and I'll enter our contact information into your phone. Then you can text him the picture. Maybe our facial recognition program will identify them."

Carter calmed my nerves, and he recognized it. He took my phone from me, entered the information, then handed it back. Both men have such calming qualities about them. No wonder they make outstanding detectives.

Night fell, and I enjoyed reading. It felt nice doing something normal. Carter never commented about boredom. He read too and watched sports on his phone.

At 3:00 am, I bolted upright. Carter stood at the door, peering through the window glass with his phone to his ear. He spoke so low that I couldn't hear, but something wasn't right.

"Carter, what's happening? What was that noise?" I asked as I fought my body to stop shaking.

He glanced at me, then said, "someone shot the bed in your previous room. The security officers are chasing the guy through the hospital now. We're on lockdown, and Blaine is on his way."

Carter saw me shaking, and he approached the bed. My state conflicted him because he wanted to reach out and hold me, but he was unsure if he should. So, he rubbed my arm, consoling me.

His voice wasn't as soothing as Blaine's, but just his presence helped. I heard more racket and braced for the aftermath. Carter took three long steps and stood at the door with his gun aimed upward.

He was clearly okay with shooting whoever entered the room. I just hoped he identified them first. I watched his eyes shift as he surveyed the hallway. "What's happening out there, Carter?"

"Nothing that I can see." Then he grinned, stepping away from the door.

He opened it while glancing down the hallway. Blaine entered in a rush. "You're safe. The security guard lost the guy in the parking deck. Also, I ran the picture you sent me through facial recognition, and we got zip. So either he has no criminal record, or the black sunglasses discouraged a match."

"Swell." I leaned my head back on the pillow and sighed. While I didn't want to feel sorry for myself, I couldn't think of anything else to do. Locked in a hospital room is not the greatest feeling because I brace for the unexpected every time someone enters.

Blaine and Carter stood at the door discussing the situation. Carter stepped through the door, leaving us alone. Then Blaine shared, "Carter will assist the security personnel with the video footage of the bad guys. They could be on video in two places. We should have a photo today. I've asked the other detectives to check in with their CIs. If something big is happening in our area, we want to know about it."

"Do you have a lot of murders in the mountains?" I asked, because it sounded like a decent question.

"No. It's been years since someone died up there. We have our fair share of missing folks, which is understandable, but not murder."

I paused and stammered, "I wonder who they killed."

"We want to know that, too. Once we get you back on your feet, we'll return to the scene. I'm unsure what we'll find there because of the weather, but we need to see it."

Nodding, I looked down at my leg and wondered if I could wiggle my toes. Every so often. I tried it. Today has been the best day so far. The pain has subsided to a manageable level, giving me the chance to try movement. Each time I move it, pain courses through the muscle, making me wonder just how serious my leg injury could have been without treatment.

Blaine had a troubled expression, like he was considering his options but unsure what to do. "What are you thinking about, Blaine?"

"What to do with you?" He looked at me, then he smiled. "Your doctor wants to move you to rehab, but I can't guard you in there, and you would jeopardize more folks."

I grinned because I was concerned it was something bad. "That isn't so terrible. The answer is no rehab. I'll rehab at home. I have a gym in the basement."

"You're not going to Colorado Springs, remember? You told me you'd stay here until we caught these guys. Have you changed your mind?" Blaine asked with a strange expression.

"No, I haven't changed my mind, but if I can't go to rehab and I can't go home, where does that leave me?"

"Staying with me if you're up for it." Blaine's eyes pleaded with me to say yes, but I was unsure if I could. Should I stay with someone I know very little about?

But something drew me to him. "What will your wife say when I show up on your arm?" I wanted to take back the question after I said it, but I couldn't, so I waited for the answer.

He paused. "There is no wife or girlfriend."

"Well, then, I guess I'm staying with you." I shrugged my shoulders because I had nowhere else to go until these killers were behind bars.

Blaine's face softened when he realized I had agreed to stay with him. We heard someone outside the door. Blaine moved to the window, peering through the glass. He grinned, unlocked the door, and opened it wide for Carter. Then another man followed.

Tears sprang to my eyes when Captain Swank entered the room. He didn't stop to meet Blaine. Instead, he walked to me, wrapping me in a bear hug. "Celeste, I couldn't wait to see you for myself. Thanks, guys, for taking care of her. She's had a run of bad luck lately."

"Yes, sir. We know. Nice to meet you, Captain Swank. I'm Detective Blaine Crosby, and this is Detective Carder Eden." They shook hands, and the detectives gave the captain and me some space.

We spoke for a while, and I explained my reasons for staying with Blaine. Captain Swank raised his right eyebrow as he questioned that decision. But after I explained it, Swank understood but felt he could protect me, too. When I mentioned he was down to two detectives, Swank agreed with me, but requested an update regularly.

He hugged me again, then left my side. But before exiting, he stood off to the rear of the room and spoke with Blaine and Carter for several minutes.

Once he left, the detectives walked to my bedside. "Your husband must have been something. Captain Swank considers you part of the family, so now he's threatened us," Then the guys laughed. Blaine added, "but I agree with you staying here, too. So, we'll take care of you or have to look that man in his eye and explain what happened, and neither of us wants to do that."

"Good. I'm glad that's settled. Did you find anything in the videos, Carter?" I asked, trying to move this case along.

He pulled a photo from a file folder. "This is the best picture we have. Each time, the guy wore a dark cap pulled low and sunglasses, but this one, the guy lowered the glasses to read something on his phone. It's only a partial, but it's the best we have."

I compared the photo with the man's face on my cell phone. "It's a match, guys. The man in the hospital was the same man on the mountain."

Both detectives stared at me. They had their answer. If this is the same guy, what do they think I know? Why do they feel the need to silence me?

Someone knocked on the door, and everyone froze. Blaine took the lead but relaxed when he recognized Nurse Hundy. "Hi, Alena, come in." He closed the door once she was safely inside.

Alena and Carter shared a glance, hoping to keep it from me. I waited until Carter stepped away, since I knew Alena would lift my bedcovers to change my bandage. Then I asked, "so, has he called you yet?"

A faint redness crept up her neck, ending at her cheeks. "No, he hasn't. Your wound looks good, Celeste. I would expect a two-day stay without medication; if you handle it okay, the doctor will release you. Do you have a way to get home?"

"I'm not going back to Colorado Springs right now. It looks like I'll stay with Detective Crosby for a while. They want to solve the case before letting me go home." I watched Alena swab medicine on my incision, and then I heard her mumble.

"What? I didn't hear you."

"Oh, nothing. You'll need exercises so you can strengthen your leg. I'll make sure the doctor provides those. Maybe I'll stop by too." She winked at me. I chuckled too.

"What are you ladies laughing about?" Carter inquired because he suspected we spoke of him.

"The fact I can't go home, and Blaine offered to let me stay with him." I watched Blaine's expression, and he never blushed. This man was serious. He wanted me to stay with him.

Carter nodded, then added in a terse tone, "it's best if you stay here. Blaine is the second best on the force, so you'll be taken care of."

I muttered, "second best? Who's first?" Alena figured it out before me, and she pointed to Carter.

"Me." Then everyone broke out into laughing fits.

Blaine's ringing phone brought our enjoyment to an end. When he answered, his face turned dark. We waited for his call to end. When he did, it shocked us. "That was Captain Jancey. They received a report from someone hearing a gunshot in the mountains, not too far from your cabin. He's sending the SWAT team to check on it. We're to stay here."

Alena's hand rushed to her mouth while no one offered a reply. Finally, Carter walked to Alena's side while Blaine stood beside me, rubbing my arm.

Chapter 3

Blaine and Carter shared a glance over at my bed. I couldn't read their expressions, but I knew they expected to hear of more death. So, who is killing folks on the mountain and why? It's time I get out of this hospital bed because I'm a sitting target.

"Blaine, can we speak with the doctor about my release? Neither of you can stay here guarding me when there's a killer on the loose." My eyes shifted from Blaine to Carter to Alena, waiting for a reply.

Then Alena said, "Celeste, you still have a couple more days of your hospital stay. You have had serious surgery, and using your leg could destroy your recovery so far."

"I get it, Alena. Being a nurse, I've seen the ramifications of those that don't follow the doctor's instructions. So I can promise I'll do everything I can to keep from using my leg."

She nodded and excused herself. After she cleared the doorway, I prodded, "so what are you two thinking? I didn't want to ask in front of Alena, but you have an idea."

They hesitated, then Blaine said, "we've heard chatter that a Mexican drug boss is in Denver and moving our way. If you disagree with paying them, they kill you with no questions. This guy is associated with multiple deaths in Denver and Los Angeles, but no one has found enough evidence to arrest him."

"Until now. I'm your evidence." I cringed when I heard them explain the killings. People like this don't stop until they handle all loose ends, and I'm a loose end. With my head back on the pillow, I wondered if I was safe anywhere.

Blaine suggested I rest while he and Carter discussed their options. I felt sure I would be the topic of their conversation, but I didn't resist. Instead, I ran scenarios through my mind, too. The first thing that popped in was my gun. I'd left everything at the cabin.

"So that you know. As soon as I'm released, I want to return to the cabin where I stayed. My items are still there." Blaine nodded his understanding but said nothing as Carter spoke.

Two hours passed before Blaine received a call alerting them to another potential murder. They never found a body, but the SWAT members found blood spatter and drag marks. They swabbed the blood and ran a DNA test to see if they could identify the deceased.

When Blaine finished explaining his call, Carter questioned the murder. "Where did the person go if they found blood and drag marks? Did they find vehicle tracks? The way Celeste described the area, it's too far to carry a dead person to a car. So they must have had a different mode of transportation."

I tried to remember my time in the woods. "I never saw or heard anything except the helicopter. When they tried to shoot me from the copter, that's when the rock fragment penetrated my leg."

"Helicopter? Can you describe it? We'll check with the closest airport and see if a copter matching your description flew from there." Carter added, hoping for something to identify this copter.

"Oh wow. I only saw it for a few seconds. The man hanging from the side door wore black sunglasses like the ones in my picture. The helicopter might have been dark blue or black. It had red writing on the side, but I don't remember the words."

"That's good, Celeste," Carter said as he and Blaine jotted notes in their small notebooks.

Blaine said, "Carter, take a few hours away from here. See what you can find out about this helicopter. That might be our best lead yet."

Carter nodded, then said on his way out the door, "tell Alena I'll be back." Then he winked.

Blaine and I chuckled, then Blaine said, "I think he likes Alena."

"Me too. She likes him too."

A few quiet moments passed between us when Blaine said, "I've arranged for you to stay in a safe house. These guys are pros, and we must be ready. Carter and I will be there, but so will other unit members. It will take us all to bring these killers to justice, but our commitment to doing just that is strong."

"Are you sure I shouldn't go home? It would save you all the trouble." I asked with uncertainty in my eyes and voice.

Blaine's head swung from side to side as he said, "I want you to stay here."

His words surprised me, so I nodded because I couldn't form the words I wanted to say. Then his phone sounded, giving me a reprieve from the conversation.

The last I remember was Blaine answering his call. When I awoke, I was alone. That's the first time that's happened since Blaine found me in the woods. My phone beeped, drawing me back to the present. Hazel texted me a half hour ago, checking on my recovery. I couldn't believe I didn't hear the first text.

I replied with an update and told her about the safe house and staying with Blaine and Carter. She made me feel good when she said those two guys are the best. Then I wondered how she knew that.

The door eased open, and Blaine peeked inside. He grinned when I waved. "How was your nap?"

"Good. What's going on, now?" I pointed to the door.

"Alena was here to let me know the doctor will be by shortly to remove your IVs and check your incision. If he feels you're good to go, he'll release you in the morning. But she reiterated you cannot use your leg until given the okay and must adhere to their strict guidelines."

"I will. Now, I must survive until tomorrow." I said as I glanced out the window.

"Now, come on, Celeste, you know you'll be fine. We've got this." Blaine stated with enthusiasm.

"Yeah, I know. Hazel told me you two were the best."

"Did she tell you how she knows that?"

I shook my head, hoping to hear the story. Blaine obliged. "A drunk truck driver that was down on his luck from a gambling trip robbed the truck stop. When law enforcement arrived, he took the workers hostage. Hazel was one. Carter and I arrived shortly after the first officers. While the officers tried to contact the truck driver, we entered the back of the store, getting the employees outside before the truck driver knew they were gone." He grinned as he described the scene.

"No wonder she says you're the best. You both saved her life."

"We eat with her at every opportunity. She's one of the good ones."

Blaine allowed Alena to enter the room after her knock. "Celeste, I'm here to remove your IVs and check your bandage. The doctor wants to see how you do overnight. Then he'll give his last word in the morning."

"Let's get these out, then." I lifted my arm for her to remove the IV, and that only took a few seconds. Then we moved to the leg. This time Blaine didn't turn around when Alena raised my gown to my thigh.

She removed the bandage and examined the incision. "A few of your stitches are loose already, and that's a sign of healing. It will please the doctor to see that."

Once she finished, she stepped outside, closing the door behind her. "Well, that was good news."

But before I could finish my statement, we heard screaming and yelling from the hallway. Blaine pressed his face to the glass and then uttered something unintelligible. "A guy has Alena by the throat holding a gun to her head."

Blaine grabbed his phone and barked orders to whoever answered. Then he rushed to my side.

"Celeste, you're pale. Breathe deeply for me. No one is getting through that door."

Then Blaine's phone rang. He listened while pressing his face to the glass again. Then he told the caller he couldn't see Alena any longer. So, he cracked the door, peeking around the frame. He described the scene, which sounded chaotic. We heard yelling, and then a door slammed.

"Where's Alena?"

"The guy forced her into the stairwell." Blaine reached up and rubbed his neck. Then he made a call.

"Carter, the guy took Alena into the stairwell on the southwest corner of the building. You know what to do." Then he dropped his phone into his pocket and leaned against the wall.

"So, now what?" I couldn't believe that was it. That man could cause Alena bodily harm, and if he did, it would be my fault. She would've been safe if she had never been my nurse.

Blaine glanced at me, "we wait." He rubbed his neck again, clearly stressed by the situation. Then he paced. Minutes ticked by without a report. Neither of us looked at the other. I watched the clouds pass the window while Blaine's footsteps sounded in the background. Every so often, he'd peer through the door's window, trying to glimpse activity, but there was none.

I jotted notes on a hospital notepad with ideas about these guys, but I was unsure if Blaine was ready to discuss them. "How about we discuss the guys and why they're here?" I said as I waited for Blaine to answer.

"Sounds good. What are your thoughts?"

"Drugs are the number one on my list. The guys I saw looked Mexican. Are drugs an extensive business this far north? I know they are in Colorado Springs."

"Haven't you heard drugs are everywhere? So, yes. We have our fair share. In fact, Carter and I have heard about a truck driver being the delivery man. But no one has inspected a truck filled with drugs. So, we think they're hiding the drugs in something. You may be onto something there. I'll circle back with Carter on that. When your predicament occurred, we changed our focus."

"While I appreciate the attention, you two must investigate the drug angle. Those two guys dressed the part. They wore dark clothing, dark hair, and dark sunglasses. If it's not drugs, then mob. I've never heard Casper mention the mob, but that doesn't mean they aren't here."

Blaine paused as he considered my thoughts. "I'm going with drugs. That fits with the rumors around town. Once we are satisfied with that idea, we'll move to the next. Carter was following up on the helicopter when Alena's situation turned dire. So, I'm unsure if he found anything yet."

We stopped talking for a moment because our thoughts returned to Alena. How much longer can she hold on if she isn't already dead? How did that guy know to grab her, or was she just in the wrong place?

When Blaine's phone blared, it startled me. Blaine said, "Carter." Then I waited as Carter explained the situation. "Okay. We'll be here when you can." Then he ended the call.

"Alena is in the emergency room getting checked out. She hit her head on the wall as the guy forced her down the stairs. It doesn't seem to be too bad. Carter shot the guy in the shoulder, but he fled the scene, and Carter refused to leave Alena. He'll join us shortly."

"These people will stop at nothing to silence me. How are we going to catch them?" By the time I had asked, Blaine had his phone to his ear.

I listened as he spoke to the security office, requesting video footage from both stairwells leading to my floor. Then he called his office asking someone to call the local pharmacies in hopes the guy needed medical supplies and such for his wound.

When the call ended, I praised Blaine for the pharmacy idea because I assumed he would seek medical attention in a hospital. But Blaine doesn't think he will. Instead, those types of killers try to remedy their injuries themselves.

Two hours later, Carter and Alena entered my room and sighed. Alena looked exhausted, but otherwise okay.

"Alena, I'm so sorry that happened to you. I hope the guy didn't hurt you besides your head."

She shook her head back and forth as she said, "no. I hit the wall when he pushed me down the steps. He tried to get into your room, but I refused to let him. Then, a patient saw him pull his gun, and she screamed. When she screamed, that's when he grabbed me. I've never been so happy to see anyone as I was to see Carter peeking out from around the corner of the parking deck. He never hesitated to shoot. The guy held my arm with one hand and his gun in the other. Carter shot him in the shoulder, and I ran when he dropped his hand to reach for his wound. I half expected a gunshot to the back, but the guy ran off in the opposite direction, and Carter escorted me to the ER."

"Way to go, partner." Blaine reached over, and the two guys exchanged a fist bump. Then they stepped away to discuss a new plan.

Alena sat in a chair beside my bed and laid her head back. "Are you okay to nap, Alena?"

"Yes, thankfully, there's no concussion. I'm just tired. The adrenaline is wearing off now." She grinned as her eyes closed.

The guys spoke for a while, then Blaine walked to my bedside. He whispered to me that Carter would stay for a few hours, but he'd return, and he looked forward to taking me to the safe house.

As he left, a niggle crept up my spine, and I wondered why. A safe house is safe, right? I shouldn't worry about those guys getting to me. Or should I?

As Alena rested, my mind ran circles. I considered my options again. If I returned to Colorado Springs, I'd bring the bad guys with me, causing more grief for more families. But if I stayed, I'd need to be prepared to protect myself. So I must return to the cabin. Either Blaine can help me get there, or Hazel will.

A door knock startled us. Carter jumped up from his chair and stood at the door with his hand on his pistol. When he opened it, it pleasantly surprised me to see my doctor. "Hey, you're early. Everything okay?"

"Yes, Celeste, it is. I've heard how good your incision looked, so I wanted to see for myself." He touched my leg as his fingers gently lifted the bandage. He nodded his satisfaction, then he changed the dressing and checked my vitals before speaking again.

"Celeste, you are free to go. I'll get the discharge papers ready for your signature. It should take two hours to process. Alena, you go home too. You deserve it."

Both of us said in unison, "thanks, Doctor."

Before the doctor left the room, Carter texted Blaine, giving him the update. But Blaine didn't respond. That caused Carter's eyebrows to bunch.

"What's wrong, Carter?" Alena asked with a touch of concern in her voice.

"Blaine always responds quickly to my text, but not this time." He didn't continue. Instead, he stared at his phone, willing it to make a sound.

I tried to make light of it by saying, "he's probably following up on a lead. I know the helicopter description intrigued him."

No one answered, so I left it at that, but the more I thought about it, the more concerned I became. Then Alena's boss asked to speak with her in the hallway. They stepped away, Carter looked at me. I saw worry etched on his forehead.

"Carter, don't worry. Blaine is fine. We discussed scenarios this morning, so he's probably following up on one." I explained because he needed to hear it. He paced, and I watched his every step.

Finally, Alena returned with a surprise. Blaine strolled inside behind her. He acted like there was nothing wrong. "Blaine, you didn't answer my text."

"Yes, I did. I was in the parking deck when it came in." Blaine pulled his phone from his pocket, then apologized. "Actually, I never hit the send button. Sorry."

"I told Celeste you always respond to texts, and something was off. Just glad it was you that was off." Carter said, laughing.

Blaine pulled a piece of paper from a folder and passed it around. "Does this look like the guy on the mountain, Celeste?"

I nodded, "absolutely, it does." Then I passed it to Alena.

"What about your guy, Alena?"

She studied it for a second, "yes, that's him." Then she handed it to Carter.

"This is the guy I shot. Do we have an ID yet?" He asked Blaine.

"No, but the captain forwarded it to the FBI. I think this is a drug cartel making waves up here, and maybe the FBI knows of it." Carter nodded.

Then another knock. This time, another nurse entered, pushing a wheelchair, and I got excited. It's about time they let me out of here.

I signed the forms in the highlighted area, then I swung my leg off the bed and grimaced. Every time I hung it down, pain shot through my body. But I was glad to be free of this hospital.

The nurse rolled me to a waiting SUV, and Blaine lifted me into the backseat. Then Alena climbed in on the other side while the men entered the front seat. I glanced around at the folks entering and leaving the hospital. Only one gave me a sideways look.

I laid my head back and enjoyed the ride until I saw Blaine study the rearview mirror. He gripped the steering wheel with both hands while Carter held the roof handle. "Guys. Do you need to share anything?" I asked as I glanced at Alena.

She gave me a shoulder shrug because she wasn't used to the signs of impending danger. I'd seen that same look on Casper. One evening, we were traveling home from supper when someone tried to force us off the road. Casper won that battle, sending the attacking vehicle headfirst into a tree. Then I worked to save the guy while we waited for the ambulance. The driver acted for someone else, and that someone had a pending court date where he tried to keep Casper from testifying.

I let the memory flood my mind, but when Blaine told us to hold on, the memory left. Carter looked into his side mirror, then relaxed. "The car didn't turn with us."

Blaine nodded, but he still kept a watchful eye on the road. I tried to think of other thoughts, but I couldn't because they returned to the cabin, and my things were still there. My gun was hidden, but there were only so many places you could hide anything in a one-room cabin. I didn't mind losing my clothes, but the gun was special.

Several minutes later, Blaine turned onto a neighborhood street with houses on both sides of the road. The houses were nice too. Most were craftsman style with porches and massive columns. He made two turns, ending in a cul-de-sac. The safe house sat in the middle of two houses.

Blaine climbed out first, handed me my crutches, then he went to the rear and gathered my bag. Carter and Blaine entered the house first, cleared it, then permitted us to enter. Whoever decorated the home has excellent taste. The family room boasted neutral colors with a grand fireplace. Then I hobbled around until I found the kitchen, and it was breathtaking. Solid surface counters in leathered granite and stainless everywhere. A massive kitchen island was large enough for four adults to eat at the bar.

"This is impressive, Blaine. What is your department doing with a safe house like this?"

He paused, "it's the FBI's. They maintain it, but we can use it if the need arises."

I nodded. Then Alena added, "if I ever need a safe house, this is the one I want." Everyone chuckled as she stood in awe of her surroundings.

"Celeste, there's a bed and bath on the lower level, so I'll stash your things in there."

"Thanks. I noticed the backyard. Can I go outside, or should I stay inside?"

"If you must venture outdoors, take someone with you. You're in no condition to fight off anyone." Blaine instructed. "I must let you know a female FBI agent is coming to sit with you for a while. Our unit is meeting to discuss the situation. I'll be back later bringing food. Tomorrow, Carter and I will drive you to the cabin. We'll retrieve your vehicle and your things."

Finally, I had my answer, and it gave me a sense of relief. I hobbled to my room, breathing deeply as pain radiated down my leg. There's no need to let the group know how badly I hurt. I have no intention of returning to the hospital.

I had a gazillion missed calls when I plucked my phone from my pocket. Captain Swank was a big part of that, and my co-workers filled the rest. After

I propped myself up on the bed using every pillow I could find, I called Swank first and then the others. My co-workers heard about my altercation and wanted to check on me and hear the details.

I had just finished my calls when I heard a soft knock on my door. "It's open."

Then Blaine peeked his head inside. "FBI Agent Sarasota is here. Do you want her to come in here?"

"Yes, please."

Blaine turned away for a moment, then Agent Sarasota appeared. We were around the same age with similar features and coloring. I glanced at Blaine, and he knew what I thought, lifting his right shoulder.

After the introductions, Blaine drove Carter and Alena back to town, leaving me with Agent Lynn Sarasota. She checked the house. Then she returned to my room. Lynn sat in the corner chair, giving her a visual of the door and the front yard.

We chatted about my ordeal then she wanted the details of my leg injury. She grimaced when I explained how the rock penetrated veins and an artery. Then I told her I was a nurse in Colorado Springs.

"My parents live in Colorado Springs. That's a nice place. I see your ring. Where's your husband?"

I paused before I answered, but I eventually told her that story, too. Her eyes grew wide by the time I finished.

"Celeste, I didn't know. My condolences for your loss. You've had a lot happen over the last few months. Maybe we can catch these folks and let you back home." The agent's cell phone beeped with a text.

While she replied to her text messages, I pondered the idea of not returning home. Maybe I needed a new start somewhere else. Could this be my new home? Alena said earlier that her hospital needed nurses.

I dosed for a while, thinking about the possibility of relocating. But then, I was unsure how Blaine felt about me. Somewhere during my dream, I waited it out to see what transpired as this case moved forward. I can't stay out of work forever, so I'd have to decide shortly.

Agent Sarasota was gone when I awoke, and Blaine sat in the chair. It was frightening when people came and went without a sound. "Hey," Blaine said in a soft tone.

"Hey. What time is it?" Blaine checked the time on his phone. When he told me, I sat up in bed.

"I slept too long. If it's suppertime now, I'll never sleep tonight." It irritated me, but then I felt my leg twitch, and I calmed. Sleep works wonders for recovery. It's your body's way of helping itself.

"You'll be fine when you take a pain pill tonight. I have supper. Can you eat?" Blaine offered.

I nodded as I reached for my crutches. "I'll join you in a minute." Then I went to the bathroom to freshen up, and when I glanced in the mirror, I was taken aback by my appearance. I still sported dark circles under my eyes, which I've never had before. Without makeup, you can only do so much.

Blaine stood at the stove with his back to me as I worked my way to the kitchen bar. He prepared a delicious meal for us, and I gobbled up every bite. Then we enjoyed our night sitting in front of the television until we got sleepy.

The following morning, Carter arrived around nine with a smile plastered on his face. "What gives with the smile?" I asked because I suspected it had to do with Alena.

"Alena and I shared a meal last night, and it was spectacular. I'm sorry this happened to you, but I wouldn't have met Alena without you. So, thank you." He patted me on the shoulder.

Blaine acted as if he wanted to add to the comments but refrained. Instead, he instructed me that we would leave in ten minutes for the cabin. So, I hobbled off to the bathroom.

When I returned, the men were in deep conversation, but it wasn't heated. So, I joined them. Blaine met my eyes first, "Celeste. You'll stay in the car until we clear the cabin. Here."

I looked down as he gave me his backup weapon. Then it hit me. "Do you two think these guys know where I was staying? I was miles from the cabin when I saw them."

"We have no way of knowing, but we're not taking chances," Carter answered as Blaine's eyes bore into mine.

We loaded into Carter's unmarked car and headed for the cabin. I was eager to see if everything remained as I left it. If it was, then no one entered the cabin in my absence.

The sun shone through the car window, making me groggy, but I refused to give in to sleep. There was too much at stake. I glanced behind us every few minutes, ensuring no one followed us. We slowed when we turned from the main road onto a one-lane road that dropped us off at the cabin. This road was wide enough for only one car. I never met another car on it when I arrived, but I'd swear I saw tracks.

"Guys, those look like tire tracks to me." I pointed over to the front seat, showing them what I referenced.

"Yeah. We saw them too. Someone has been here." Blaine's worst fear just showed. Then he added, "remember the drill. You stay inside the locked car while we clear the cabin." I watched them walk to the cabin until they went out of sight.

Then I waited for the guys to return for me.

Chapter 4

I clicked the doors locked after the guys exited the vehicle. They left the key fob with me, so I could tap the alarm button if I had an issue.

Since Blaine parked away from the cabin for safety, I only saw the cabin's rear from my location. Unfortunately, I parked my car at the front door. A shadow passed the window, then the curtain moved. A face appeared, looking at me.

Blaine didn't wave. Instead, he stepped away from the window. Then I wondered why he wouldn't let me enter the cabin. Finally, after several minutes had passed, Blaine approached the car.

I unlocked it, and he opened the door. "They flattened two tires on your car, so I'll have it towed to the police department. One of our service guys will replace them. Everything inside looks okay. Do you want to go inside to gather your things?"

"I'd like to if it's okay with you." I pleaded with him to let me go into the cabin. This cabin helped me work through my husband's death. I wanted to see it one more time. Blaine took my crutches, then helped me stand on the uneven ground.

The trek to the door was slow. First, it made for a tricky walk between the uneven ground and the dampness. Then the stairs were more challenging than I expected. But I managed. I inhaled deeply when I crossed the threshold.

Blaine saw emotion spread across my face, so he and Carter stepped onto the porch. As I circled the cabin, I grabbed my things and took interior pictures. Then I snapped photos from every window. When I look back on these pictures, I'd remember how far I'd come in life and the experiences that brought me here.

"Blaine, Carter!" I screamed.

They rushed to my side. Then I pointed through the window to the sky.

Blaine scooped me up into his arms. "Carter, get the crutches and her bag. Let's go."

"Wait. I stashed my gun under the bed on the second wooden slat from the top." The copter was louder now, and I hung onto Blaine's neck.

Carter lifted the mattress with one arm, grabbed the gun, stuffed it into my bag, then we fled the cabin. We rounded the cabin's corner just as gunfire sounded over our heads. Blaine lowered his head as he ran, protecting me from the bullets.

Blaine slid me into the backseat, then raced to climb in the passenger seat. Carter had the vehicle in drive when Blaine shut his door. The car shimmied as Carter reversed out of the tight spot. He made a three-point turn and drove us back to town.

"Lay in the seat, Celeste. Look out the windows for the helicopter." Carter suggested.

I couldn't find the helicopter because of the trees, which I thought was good because that meant they couldn't see us either. But I didn't hear the helicopter either.

"How come I don't hear it anymore?" I asked with my eyes on the sky.

Blaine replied, "that concerns us too. We hope the helicopter doesn't land on the road, blocking our escape."

Then Carter added, "we have two more miles of this road, then it opens. Call dispatch and have them send a unit our way."

I listened to Blaine describe our situation to a 911 dispatcher. She was calm and took the information without question. "How long until your backup arrives?"

The radio answered for me, "ETA three minutes."

"We'll get there before our backup does, right?" I asked.

Blaine nodded and didn't offer words of encouragement. This situation worried them, and they didn't want to scare me. Little did they know it was too late for that. I wanted the trip to the cabin to be easy, but the helicopter showed.

I wondered if those guys had surveilled the cabin this whole time, hoping I would return. But, since they couldn't get to me in the hospital, they waited in the next best place.

"I have an idea. If the helicopter sits in our path, I'll take a picture. Maybe that will help us identify it."

No one answered me. "Can I sit up yet?"

"No!" the guys barked in unison.

I lay in the backseat studying the clouds as they passed, wondering if I'd see them tomorrow. A helicopter against a car. I don't see this ending well without help. The car slowed, and I kept my questions to myself because Blaine and Carter knew what they were doing, and I had to trust them. But that didn't stop me from wanting to know what was happening.

Carter asked, "how do you want to play this?"

Blaine looked out the windows, searching for the helicopter. "They've landed on our road around the next bend. They have far more firepower than we do. Let's get the rifles from the trunk. Then, if we have to, we can unleash a barrage of bullets into the helicopter. Maybe that will hamper them."

The car stopped, and I didn't budge. Blaine jumped from the passenger seat, trotted to the trunk, and removed their rifles and extra ammunition. Then he slammed the trunk lid so hard it jarred my teeth.

Carter took a rifle from Blaine, and both guys loaded the guns. Then they readied an extra magazine for their pistols. While they prepared their weapons, I pulled mine from my bag. I double-checked the bullets just to make sure they were still there. Then I realized I didn't bring extra ammunition.

The car inched forward when the radio sounded. Our backup was thirty seconds away. Carter floored the car, sliding around the corner. The guys were right because the helicopter sat in the road's middle with its rotor still turning. They were ready to kill us and then fly away.

A bullet pierced the front windshield of Carter's car, halting our progress. Then another bullet struck the grill. If those guys keep shooting the car, we'll have no chance of survival. So, Carter jerked the car into reverse and smashed the pedal to the floor. Blaine's side mirror exploded as we turned around the corner.

Then the radio crackled. "Crosby, Eden. This is Miller. There's a helicopter on the road."

"Shoot it. And shoot whoever emerges from the helicopter. Stay in your vehicle. Back away from the copter and use your rifle." Carter instructed. Then he said, "I'm going on foot."

Blaine looked at me, "go with him." I suggested.

As the doors opened and closed, I sat up. Then I realized I could see nothing because Carter drove us away from the copter. Gunfire rang out as the men exchanged bullets with the crooks. Finally, the copter people grew tired of the gunfight and climbed onboard. As the helicopter lifted from the ground, three officers shot at it. Some bullets hit the machine while others continued their path into the sky.

Carter and Blaine trotted back to the car, and I breathed a sigh. Then the radio crackled. "Crosby, Eden. You there?"

Blaine replied, "yeah, Miller. Thanks for the backup."

"Anytime, but your copter left here smoking out on the right side. So someone must have hit the motor. Want me to track it?" Miller asked.

"10-4. We're coming out now."

Carter pressed the pedal, hoping our car remained operational after the gunshot. It choked twice, but then the motor roared to life. Since I lived through this gunfight, I'm unsure if I'll ever return to the cabin. I need a place with multiple escape routes.

We stopped at the truck stop so Blaine and Carter could meet with Miller. I found Hazel and got a big hug. We enjoyed coffee together as I described the latest attack. Then I said, "once this is all behind me, we're getting together when it's safe." We hugged again and promised to stay in touch.

Miller told the guys about the copter and how it flew west, away from town. Then Carter asked, "What's west? There's no airport to the west. There are only more mountains and forest land."

Then Blaine, "how far could they have gone with a smoking motor?"

"Depending on the damage, they couldn't have flown until they ran out of gas. A bullet will render the helicopter useless if it strikes the optimum location. If a bullet glances off the motor, it might smoke, but it wouldn't cause catastrophic failure." Miller showed us the knowledge of flying that he gained from the service.

"Great. So, the copter could be anywhere."

"Precisely," Miller stated. "But the copter looked personal. Not business owned. There was no logo, and the numbers were on the belly. But even if it's owned personally, the pilot would still need clearance to fly. So the copter wouldn't have a hangar at an airport. Instead, the pilot would land it at home with a huge outbuilding."

"Interesting. Thanks, Miller. So, instead of searching for the copter at airports, we need to check satellite footage around the area." Blaine said as he shared a glance with me.

A pause gave the team time to absorb this newest information. Then, Carter suggested, "let's get to the safe house, then we'll work on the satellite imagery."

As we drove to the safe house, Carter made several unnecessary turns. He made sure no one followed us to the house. Then he pulled the car into the garage, closing the door before we exited the vehicle.

They armed the house with a state-of-the-art security system. Blaine passed through several layers before the lock clicked open for us. Carter went directly to the front windows, checking the road, while Blaine did the same in the back.

When I heard nothing, I lay on the bed, willing my leg to stop hurting. The pain has subsided somewhat but returns with a vengeance when I'm on it for long durations. Blaine knocked on the door before entering.

"Everything okay?"

"Yeah. I just had to rest for a little while." Blaine saw the pain in my face and approached the bed.

"You did too much. We've been here for a while now. Carter and I will be here working on the satellite imagery. If you need anything, just yell. No need to get up." He winked, then left.

As I dosed, I wondered how I got myself into this. When I saw those men in the field, I knew they were up to no good. I should have turned and run as fast as I could have given the terrain. But I didn't. Instead, I heard the gunshot. Then I took a picture of them. I'll never get over the sound of that gunshot in the mountains. The echo was incredible.

I awoke to someone mumbling. It sounded like they were speaking on the phone. If it were necessary, they'd wake me. When no one knocked on the door, I fell asleep again, except this time I dreamed. Helicopters swooped over my head, and as I ran, dodging their blows.

The next thing I remember is Blaine shaking me. "Celeste, wake up. You're dreaming."

When I opened my eyes, Blaine stared back at me. Then the tears flowed. The dream was so real I couldn't stop the tears. Finally, Blaine pulled me in for a hug, and I laid my head on his shoulder. The tears finally slowed enough for me to pull back. It embarrassed me. I had screamed out in my sleep but I didn't remember doing that. But I'd never been traumatized either.

"Sorry." I stammered, looking down at my hands.

"There's nothing to be sorry for. You had a dream, and it was frightful, but you're okay now." He rubbed my arm as he waited for a reply.

"It was the scariest dream I'd ever had." He leaned over and kissed my forehead. When I looked up at him, I threw back the bedcovers, reaching for my crutches. "Where are you going?" Blaine asked.

Pointing to the bathroom, he chuckled as he helped me stand. I hobbled off, and he left the room. I needed the space, and this was the best place. Glancing in the mirror, I rubbed the spot where he kissed me. Was that just a friendly peck, or did it mean something entirely different?

Carter stood at the coffee pot when I entered the kitchen. "Hey, Celeste. Want some coffee?"

"I would love a cup." I walked over to the counter, poured creamer and sweetener into my cup, then looked down at my crutches. Blaine walked up behind me, reached around me, taking my cup.

"I got this. Come on. I have news."

After I sat, Blaine handed me my coffee, and the heat felt good in my hands. "What's the news?"

"The DNA test came back from the blood spatter at the mountain. The blood is from two different people. They're still working to determine the race of one while another showed in CODIS. That person is Nathaniel Bisgrove. He's a twenty-nine-year-old lifelong criminal. Nathaniel has been in and out of jail for most of his life, starting at age fourteen. His last known address was in Denver. We've asked the Denver police to do a welfare check for us. He's also on parole, so I left a message for his parole officer."

"That's great news. Finally, we have a potential name for a victim. What's he been in jail for?"

"Drugs. He's been a low-level drug dealer until two years ago. Then Denver's drug unit put him on their radar about nine months ago when they spotted him with a known drug leader out of Mexico."

Then Carter added, "we suspect Nathaniel skimmed off the top of a drug deal, and the drug leader made a statement to the other runners."

I nodded because it made sense. But why kill them in the mountains? Did they think no one would hear it or see it? The area they chose was the most remote part of the mountain. "Did the killers land their helicopter nearby where they shot Nathaniel? They were in an open field. I went back to the field for more pictures, and I'm certain I didn't see the entire space. When you view my pictures, the field continues in the background."

Carter and Blaine faced one another. "She's good, Blaine." Blaine grinned and agreed.

"I was just married to a cop and learned how to think like one," I stated as I shrugged my shoulders. Then I realized I spoke of my marriage without crying. Baby steps.

"That would explain how come we saw no vehicle tracks. The drag marks the SWAT team found ended in the field. Maybe they dragged the victim to their helicopter, then disposed of the body somewhere."

"Yeah, and we may never find the bodies," Carter explained.

I sipped my coffee, thinking about the new information, and it seemed plausible. But why bring the victims this far when people are murdered every day in the deepest, darkest areas of the city? It would have been just one more unsolved murder if they had handled it appropriately.

The guys worked their computers as I stared at a muted television. Nothing held my attention these days. I wondered what I could do to stay busy. Then, plucking my phone from my pocket, it vibrated with a text message.

I read it and grinned. Then I dialed. "Hey Anita, it's me, Celeste."

The guys glanced my way, but when they saw the phone to my ear, they returned to the satellites. I talked on the phone for thirty minutes, discussing my predicament, my injury, and my timetable for returning to work.

When our call ended, I noticed how good it felt to talk with someone from home, but then I wondered if I could ever return. That place had many memories, not terrible ones, just life-changing ones.

"Blaine, look at this structure. Is it large enough to accommodate a helicopter?" But before Blaine answered, Carter's cell phone blared.

Grinning, he answered. The caller spoke as Carter listened. Then he said, "I'm glad they shifted you to the ICU. If anything changes, let me know. See you soon." Then he ended the call.

He shared that the hospital assigned Alena to the ICU as a precaution. The hospital administrators didn't want her working on an open floor since her ordeal.

Then Blaine answered, "I believe it is. What are the coordinates? We can ask Captain Jancey to send a team to check it out."

Carter provided the coordinates, then Blaine called their captain. While Blaine spoke to the Captain, Carter interrupted. Blaine placed his phone on speaker, then turned the conversation over to Carter. "Captain, I found another similar building. But with the surrounding trees, I'm unable to find a residence. It appears the buildings sit alone in a cleared section of land. Can we find the property owner?"

"I think we should. That might tell us what we need to know. I'll get back to you." The captain ended the call, and they gave each a fist bump.

With the buildings and the property owner identified, we might solve this case quicker than I expected. Then I'd have to decide my future, and I wasn't sure I was ready for that.

I wanted to see the backyard, so I eased myself through the back door and onto the deck. The sun remained in the sky, but it sat low, giving a cooler feel to the temperature. I wanted a hot cup of coffee but didn't want to bother the guys, so I huddled in a chaise and stared out over the backyard.

The house backed up to a forest area, but it wasn't dense, so I could see for a good distance. There was a twelve-foot-tall privacy fence surrounding the yard, but with the deck, you could view the woods easily. Small animals skittered through the woods, searching for food. Then I saw movement, and it wasn't an animal.

That's when I groaned, knowing I couldn't move fast. So instead, I texted Blaine, alerting them to the movement in the woods. The door opened within seconds. Blaine picked me up from the chair, toting me inside and placing me on the sofa, away from the windows.

Carter took a position at one window while Blaine took another. Together they scoped out the backyard. As Carter peered through the blinds, he asked, "is there a way around the house from the backyard?"

Blaine's head snapped around. Then he trotted to the front window. "I see nothing. Celeste, did the movement sound or looked like an animal?"

I thought back to what I'd seen. "I never saw a person or animal. The large bush moved, then I heard walking where twigs snapped. It sounded too loud to be an animal. But if it were a person, you'd think they wouldn't have been so loud if they tried to sneak up on us." Then I shrugged my shoulders. Maybe I overreacted.

The guys let the tension out of their shoulders, but their concerns remained. Finally, Blaine shared, "I'm going to check out the bush."

"You stay here with Celeste. I'll go." Carter said as he reached for the door. You can watch me from the deck.

He left through the front door and turned left, following the fence to the back. We saw the top of his head as he stopped and listened. Then he proceeded to the bush. It moved as he approached. Carter lifted his weapon, then used his foot to open the bush. When two cottontail rabbits jumped out, Carter jumped back too, almost falling.

I stood at the window with Blaine on the deck. Carter's surprise at the rabbits was priceless. He returned with a red face, shaking his head. We laughed when he plopped down on the sofa. "Those were the biggest rabbits I've ever seen. They must have lived back there sheltered."

"That was the funniest thing I've seen in a long time. Thanks for checking on things for us." Then I offered my thanks too.

Jancey called Blaine, and he placed the phone on speaker. "We have the buildings in sight with a surveillance team. Unfortunately, we've not found the owners because they titled the land in a company that is several layers deep. I'm searching for a judge that will sign a warrant for the building based on the helicopter, but I'm coming up empty. Maybe we'll get something from the surveillance teams."

"Ok. Thanks for the update. We'll search again for buildings just in case those don't work."

When the call ended, Carter's phone sounded. He found a quiet place to answer, and Blaine winked at me. We knew the caller. Then Carter looked at us with a strange expression. The call ended abruptly.

Carter shared, "that was Alena. A nurse in the ER heard that someone found a human skull on a walking path near your cabin."

"How did a nurse hear that before we did?" Blaine inquired, confused.

"An officer brought in an injured suspect, and the call sounded from his radio while he stood in the exam room." She called Alena, and Alena called me.

Blaine quickly dialed Jancey. He didn't answer, so he left a message. Then he dialed Hudson, another team member. He answered but sounded strained.

Carter glanced at Blaine. Then Blaine asked about the human skull. Hudson explained, "what we know so far is a hiker found a human skull on a walking path. It's in terrible shape, though. The way the caller described it, it's possible a bear caused the damage. We're on our way to the scene now. I'll call you back soon."

"Thanks, Hudson."

Then I added, "do you think that's Nathaniel?"

Blaine and Carter nodded, then Blaine replied, "we'll know for certain if we can ID the skull, or we wait for the lab test."

Silence overtook us as thoughts raced through our minds. A surveillance team watched buildings we suspected of holding a helicopter, and now someone found a human skull. How much longer than this craziness last?

Blaine paced, and Carter texted with someone, presumably Alena, while we waited for word on the skull. I hope it isn't another murder, but these people are relentless, so nothing should come as a surprise.

When Blaine's phone rang, it startled us. He tapped the speakerphone so we could join in the conversation. "Hudson. We're all here. What did you find?"

"It's a skull, and it's been in the elements for a while. At first glance, it appears a large animal ripped the head from the body. We're searching now for the rest, and if we don't find it close by, we'll have a dog search for us." Hudson stated.

We looked at each other, knowing it couldn't be Nathaniel. "Can you tell the race of the victim?"

"No, Crosby. There's no skin left. I'm telling you, most of the meat has been chewed off."

I groaned as Hudson described the skull. Blaine laid his hand on my arm, then Carter asked, "where exactly is the skull? Do you have coordinates?"

Hudson rattled off the coordinates as we jotted them on paper. Next, we'd search the area with satellite imagery. Hudson promised to call with any new information. Then Jancey called to tell us about the skull.

When Blaine told him we already knew it, he felt cheated. But we explained how we had firsthand knowledge of the find. He understood.

Carter entered the coordinates in the satellite software, and we waited. Finally, a blue marker popped up on the screen showing the location of the skull. Then we added the coordinates for my cabin. We inhaled when we saw how close they were. They were within a half-mile of each other. Carter zoomed out on the map and pointed to the field. The skull sat between my cabin and the field where I first saw the two guys.

Blaine's and Carter's phones dinged simultaneously. They tapped the messages button, then grimaced. Hudson forwarded a photo of the skull. It had a perfect bullet hole dead center of the forehead.

"Another murder. But this one starts with a skull and no name. Where one has a name, and the body is missing, it sounds like our guys use the mountain as their killing field. That means our victims are connected. We just need to find out how." Carter explained.

"If the skull is clean, how can anyone track the rest of the body since there's no blood?" I asked.

"We have K9s that are taught to track. They track bones or blood. Once they sniff the skull, they'll know what they're after. The handler just follows the dog. With luck, the rest will be close by, but if not, the dog could walk miles." Blaine shared.

I nodded because I liked those odds. The dogs could help speed up the process for us. Then I added, "can a crime scene tech tell us how long the skull has been in the elements? I just wonder how long these guys have been working in this area."

Blaine glanced at Carter, then Carter pointed at Blaine and said, "Theo."

"Who's Theo?"

"Only the best crime scene tech on the planet. That boy is a genius in the lab." Carter said as he tapped a button on his phone. He spoke with Theo, describing the skull and our case. Theo chastised Carter for not alerting him about my case before now. Carter apologized and then asked if he had time to investigate it.

When Carter ended the call, Blaine said, "that went well," in a sarcastic tone.

"He didn't understand why we didn't call him when this mess started. I'm unsure why too. Other than the only evidence so far is the blood swabs that SWAT did for us."

Then I said, "maybe he can do something else with the blood too. If he's as good as you say." Tilting my head as I glanced at the guys.

I glanced at the house and asked, "do you think it's okay for me to go outside now? The sun is almost down, and I don't want to miss the sunset."

Both guys nodded, so I hobbled out the back door while staring at the famous bush. I wouldn't let rabbits scare me from sitting on the deck.

The men huddled over the computer and papers. They discussed something while I enjoyed the fresh air. Both had their phones to their ears, making me wonder what I missed.

Then Blaine opened the door, "they've recovered more body parts, and they don't expect to find them all. Some of the smaller bones could be between animals and the terrain. Theo will handle the tests for us tonight and provide us with whatever information he can tomorrow. I can say they believe this skull is also male, about six feet tall based on a thigh bone."

"Interesting. All male victims. What do you make of that?" I asked Blaine.

"Until we gather more information, that's hard to answer. There are so many variables here that guessing won't help us. We'll have a better direction when we find a solid lead."

Carter joined us outside. "Get this. They just found a stash of skeletons."

"A stash?" I mumbled.

"Yeah, like too many to count."

Chapter 5

Carter explained they brought in a K9 cadaver dog. The dog uncovered multiple skeletons within a mile of the skull. Someone dumped them in a single pile.

I couldn't believe my ears. Why so many deaths? Who are these people? Their families must wonder where they are. "I've worked with bones in the past. If Theo needs help, I'd be happy to work with him."

Blaine and Carter shared a glance. Then, Blaine said, avoiding a decision on that one, "let's wait until we hear from Theo. If it's too much for his lab, we might call the FBI for help."

Then Carter blurted out, "they'll take this case from us if they take the bones."

"Maybe not." Blaine countered, pacing as he reviewed the case. He used his fingers to count off ideas or evidence, and I was unsure which. Then he stepped inside, leaving Carter with me. Carter's phone dinged several times in a row. He grimaced when he clicked the photos open. "Here are the skeletons. There are a few pictures, so scroll if you want to see more."

I accepted his phone and viewed the pictures. His description was spot on when he called the find a stash. It was indeed more than one. I counted seven skulls on top, but several areas weren't visible, so I expected more underneath.

"Carter, why would someone kill so many people and dump them in a single grave?"

"The mountain is less traveled than the city, giving the killer a sense of anonymity. But, unfortunately, it appears they've used the mountain as their killing ground for years, and it probably would have never been found without you."

"That's why they keep coming after me. They're protecting what was already there." I shivered thinking about the bodies on that mountain.

"We think you stumbled onto something much larger than what we thought at the beginning. If the FBI helps with the bones, we'll be a part of the team because we have you." Carter said.

Since the sun dropped below the horizon, the temperature dropped too. Again, it was chilly, so Carter and I returned to the family room. We found Blaine sitting in front of the computer. He had markers on a map showing my cabin, the field, the skull, and the body stash.

Blaine grinned at me when I walked over. "Look at this map. Everything is within two miles. I want to check on the cabins in this area, except for yours. I've seen that one. Did you find any other cabins on your walks?"

I nodded. "I slept in the crawl space of one, but I'm unsure if I could find it again. That was during my chase."

"It's amazing you survived, Celeste, after your ordeal."

I nodded as tears formed behind my eyes. Blinking, I tried to stop them from racing down my face. Unfortunately, a few escaped before I could stop them as memories flooded my mind.

Theo called Blaine. "Guys, I'm at the body dump site. This is unreal. I'm up to eleven skulls, and I'm unsure if we've reached the bottom. This grave has been here for years. We're going to need some help with the identification of this many folks. You need to decide how you want to handle it."

Blaine replied, "I'll call Jancey. Then I'll call you back. Is Hudson with you?"

"Yeah, he's here. Do you need him?"

"I was just checking on him. Talk soon." Blaine reached over and tapped the red circle on his phone's screen. He glanced at Carter. "You said earlier that we might need the FBI. You were right."

Blaine tapped the speed dial button for Captain Jancey. We listened as he described the scene to Jancey. Blaine spoke for a few minutes before Jancey asked a question. Then Blaine replied to Jancey with, "I agree."

When their call ended, he stated, "Jancey will call the FBI."

I slipped off to my room for a nap and then to do my exercises. My leg feels better every day, but I think it will be a long time before I can jog again if I ever get there. Then I remembered I needed to check in with Captain Swank and work.

Sleep came easily, but so did the dreams. This time Casper took a backseat to the faceless killers that stalked me in the woods. They popped out from behind trees as I ran from them. I woke myself before screaming out in my sleep like yesterday. Checking the clock, I'd only been asleep for forty-nine minutes. I moaned because now I felt groggy, but I pushed myself to do my exercises. As I ground through, I could hear Blaine and Carter talk, but I couldn't understand their words. Finally, my curiosity got the best of me, so I hobbled out into the family room.

"What's happening now?"

Carter looked to Blaine. "Someone took shots at our group standing over the grave. Hudson took a bullet to the shoulder, a bullet grazed another officer on the upper arm, and Officer Miller tackled Theo just as a bullet raced over his head."

"Miller called and gave us the rundown. He had just arrived to check on the group when the first bullet tore through the group. He noticed the shooter shot people standing in a line and figured Theo would be next in line for a bullet. If Miller hadn't stopped by, Theo might be dead." Carter added as his head moved from side to side.

My blood boiled as it coursed through my veins. How can you stop someone like this? Blaine answered another call, and he ended with 10-4. "We have a copter heading their way. They carry infrared cameras, too. Maybe we'll get lucky, and they'll pick up a heat signature. Also, SWAT is on its way. They'll station themselves around Theo while he finishes his tasks."

"This is completely out of hand. What are these guys hiding?" I asked as my eyes bounced from Blaine to Carter and back.

"It must be important to go to all this trouble. Hudson's wound was a through and through, so there's no chance of recovering a bullet." Blaine replied.

Carter's eyebrows drew together. "What about the bullet that grazed the officer? It would have slowed its progress when it met flesh. So I suggest we search for that bullet. If we find it, we do the same in the field, and if they match, we can tie the shooter to the crime."

Blaine nodded. "Celeste, I'll have someone stay with you while Carter and I search for the bullet."

"You're going to the mountain where some of your guys were just ambushed?" I stared at Blaine, waiting for a response.

He nodded. "Chances are they've left the area. Especially when the helicopter arrived."

I added nothing because the guys would do whatever they wanted to anyway, so I kept my thoughts to myself. But I'm unsure if I could handle it if one of these is injured because of me. It's hard enough hearing about Hudson, but these guys have been with me day and night since Blaine found me.

After hopping to the counter, I leaned against it while sipping coffee. Blaine's phone rang, and I braced because I figured they would leave me. Instead, when his call ended, he said, "Hudson is in the ER getting patched up. He'll swing by to grab one of us and return to the mountain."

"What? After being shot, he's going back. He can't. I'm sure the doctors were against that unless he didn't tell them. If he's on pain meds, he needs to stay home." My nursing came out of my mouth so fast that I stopped when I saw their faces. Then I chuckled. "Sorry. I'm a nurse, remember? I can't imagine a band-aid would suffice for a bullet wound."

Carter chuckled, too. "From experience, they give you a pain shot in the wound so they can clean it. Then they cover it. So, technically, you have several hours before the pain meds wear off. So he might as well work while he's not feeling it because later, he won't have a choice but to slow down."

I shrugged my shoulders because I disagreed again, and there was no stopping them. So, I finished my coffee while the guys worked on the maps. Finally, they felt certain they knew where the shots originated, so they could triangulate the bullet, hoping to retrieve it from there.

Carter agreed to travel with Hudson, so he slipped off to change clothes. He wanted to be prepared for whatever situation they had met. Blaine stood beside me and said, "we're going to finish this mess, I promise."

"I know. Both of you guys are talented. That's obvious. But I don't want to see either of you injured or worse, because of me. I couldn't handle it."

Blaine didn't reply, and I didn't push him. I couldn't ask for a promise that he might not get to keep. When he returned to the kitchen, Carter spoke on the phone, ending our conversation. Then he grinned. His call ended. Then he chuckled. "That was Alena. Hudson told her I was going to the woods with him. She tried her best to stop Hudson because of the shoulder wound, but he wouldn't have it. Alena gave him some pain pills and an extra shot. He might have four hours before the feeling returns."

Then we heard a car enter the drive. My head snapped around, looking outside. Blaine bypassed me and walked to the door with his hand on his gun. When he saw the visitor, he opened the door. "Hudson."

"Crosby. How are things?"

Before Blaine could answer, Carter barked, "Hudson, let's go. We're under time constraints with that shoulder."

The guys turned and headed out. I lifted a quick prayer for their safety. Once they backed out of the drive, Blaine returned to the computer. Then he huffed.

"What's wrong?" I asked, as I hobbled to his side.

"This Denver officer keeps texting me for an update. As far as I know, he isn't working on the case, so I'm confused about his interest. Maybe I should call him. Do you know any Denver officers?"

"Not that I can think of. Casper didn't have many dealings with others outside of his office and the DEA."

This time it was Blaine's head that spun around. "DEA? I thought Casper was a detective."

"He was, but sometimes the captain would loan him out to the DEA. So why are you asking about Casper? Do you think these murders are associated with something Casper worked on before someone killed him?"

"Strange coincidence, if it's not related. First, someone ambushes your husband and his partner. Then you escape to a cabin that happens to be close to their killing field. It sounds like Casper and his partner were onto these guys. I want to discuss this with Jancey first, then Swank. Also, I need Casper's files."

I pondered Blaine's idea. "So, these guys know who I am? That's why they won't stop their attacks. Your idea sounds plausible."

Blaine had his phone to his ear when Jancey answered. I listened as they discussed Blaine's idea. Then, when the call ended, he stated, "Jancey wants to discuss this with Swank before I call. Apparently, they know one another."

Then he added, "do you have the last case your husband worked? Was it with the DEA?"

"I don't recall if it was with the DEA, but someone named Jordan called him the night before, and they spoke. Casper's tone was terse, but I didn't pry."

"Jordan. I suppose that could be a first or last name and either sex."

"I don't know that because I didn't hear the voice." Now, my pulse ticked upward. Did Casper's last case get him killed? Why didn't Swank warn me?

Jancey called back. Blaine answered and listened, then asked, "so, are we getting the file?" Then silence as Jancey replied, and Blaine nodded at me.

I was unsure if I wanted to see Casper's last file, but if it stopped this killing spree, then so be it. What makes little sense is how I spotted the guys killing that man. They wouldn't have known me had they seen me on the sidewalk. Maybe everything just ran together into a neat little pile.

Some ninety minutes later, Carter called. Blaine tapped the speaker phone, and Carter shared how they found the bullet with the laser. Now they were headed to the field to find one there. They're hoping the bullet remained in the ground, making it easier to retrieve.

"Carter, how's Hudson? He doesn't have long until his shots wear off." I inquired.

"So far, he's fine. But we know about the time constraints. We hope to finish this within the hour. Talk soon." Then he ended the call. I looked at Blaine.

"He sure got off the phone quickly. So you don't think he's hiding anything from us?"

Blaine offered no words. Instead, I received a shoulder shrug. I hope Hudson is okay to finish their quest. If they find two matching bullets, it would be solid evidence the murders are connected.

I wandered off to the deck, thinking sunshine would help my worries. But it didn't. My thoughts circled back to Casper and our shared last few days. While I couldn't recall anything specific about his work, he seemed preoccupied. Something at work could have triggered it because he kept his cases close at hand. Then I remembered being at home with Casper in his office.

He was in such deep thought he didn't hear me walk up behind him. Then, when I touched his shoulder, he jumped slightly and closed the file on his desk. Now, I wonder what was in the file.

Texting Blaine to join me, I waited because I needed to share. "Everything okay?" Blaine asked.

"I just remembered something." Then I rehashed my memory of Casper in his office. Blaine's eyes grew wide.

"Do you think the file is still at your place?"

"I have no reason to believe it's not. Unless he took it to the police department."

"Does he normally have files at home?"

"I've seen him with a few over the years. He works through scenarios when he's at home, so I think he makes his own files. But that's just a guess."

Blaine nodded as he considered the idea of visiting my house and retrieving Casper's files. "Let's see what happens here, but we might visit your house and check out Casper's office, with your permission, of course." Blaine tilted his head and lifted an eyebrow.

"Funny, Detective. You know you have access anytime you want it."

While we stared at each other, Theo called. "Hey, guys. The FBI offered their help in identifying our skeletons. It will go much faster with their involvement. They're sending an analyst to see me today. I've extracted DNA from two of the newest skeletons. After that, I'll submit to CODIS, hoping for news."

"That sounds great, Theo. Thanks for the update. Keep us posted." Blaine said as he ended the call.

"It's been an hour, and we haven't heard from Carter," Blaine advised as he tapped Carter's speed dial button. When he didn't answer, Blaine called Hudson. Neither man responded to his call. Blaine stood and paced in front of the fireplace. His hand wrapped around his neck, rubbing it.

Blaine's phone sounded, and he quickly returned to the sofa. He tapped the button and said, "Captain."

"Swank will forward Casper's file to us. Once he reviewed it, he feels this entire ordeal might be connected." Blaine glanced at me. "It appears Casper and his partner were working with the DEA on a case. They had a major drug leader in their sights when someone ambushed them."

Blaine listened to Jancey, but then he added, "Celeste remembered Casper looking at a file at their home office right before his murder. Can Swank send a car by the house just to confirm it's untouched? I'd like to visit Casper's home office. Celeste permitted us."

Jancey paused before replying, "let's see what Swank sends us. We might not need it, but who knows, it might hold information that's not in the office file. So we'll sit on this information. Are Carter and Hudson back yet?"

"No, sir, they're not. I tried to reach them by phone, but neither responded. So I'll try again." Blaine explained, trying not to sound uptight.

The call ended, and Blaine glanced my way as he pressed the button for Carter. The phone rang five times before voicemail answered. Then he did the same for Hudson. Blaine's expression caused me pain. The situation worried him, and there wasn't anything he could do sitting on the sofa with me.

"Was anyone else going with them?"

"No. They wanted it to stay under the radar instead of having a large group of people milling around. The guys assumed this would be an easy in and out with just the two of them."

"So, there's a possibility they're just busy searching for the bullet. Especially if they're sifting dirt because that's a tedious and time-consuming project." I offered.

Blaine's email alert sounded. He touched his mouse pad, and the computer came to life. "We have the file." He said as he glanced at me.

I tried not to show emotion, but I'm sure my face didn't listen to my thoughts. So while I kept the tears away, my heart pumped faster than it should have.

Blaine opened the file, perused it, then returned to another section of interest. "Celeste, would you mind looking at a few photos?"

Exhaling, I waited until Blaine slid the computer over to me so I could view it. I was appreciative that the photos were surveillance images and not of Casper. Something niggled in the back of my mind as I studied the images. But I couldn't figure out what.

"I've never seen these people before." The last picture jumped on the screen when my finger touched the forward arrow. "Hold on. Let me revisit these. I need to be looking at the people in the background. The guys we're searching for are hired killers, not the leaders."

Blaine nodded as he rechecked his phone for the umpteenth time. The more minutes that passed, Blaine became increasingly stressed with the absence of Hudson and Carter.

"This guy here. He's one guy from the field." I plucked my phone from my pocket and scrolled until I found the picture. "Here. This is the same guy."

"You're right. So, this proves that this file and those murders are connected. Now, let me read the file. Once I finish, we'll better understand what we're facing."

I leaned back in the chair, working on scenarios, too. Did Casper stumble into something unexpected, just as I did?

Blaine worked on the file for what felt like hours, but in reality, it wasn't. Since we didn't have a printer, he snipped bits and pieces of documents he wanted to keep handy. Afterward, he rechecked his phone and moaned.

"Call them again," I suggested.

He did, and both phone calls went unanswered. "Something is wrong. I need to notify the captain. Maybe he can have an unmarked unit drive up there and check on them."

"I think they're using caution. Let them work. Hudson still has an hour before the pain starts. Give them that, then call for backup." I offered as a way to calm Blaine. He liked to be in the thick of things instead of sitting on the sideline guarding a wounded woman.

Blaine accepted the instructions and reviewed the case file again. He studied the pictures, trying to determine their location. Some photos appeared to be from downtown Denver on a stretch of undeveloped land. Then he said, "I wonder if their helicopter garage is on this land."

I hobbled over to the computer, looked at it, and said, "that's going to be hard to find. Does the FBI have a computer software program that can match pictures with the actual landscape?"

"That's a great idea. But like you said, it's so bland. I wonder how many matches they'll receive."

I replied with a shoulder shrug, thinking anything was worth a try.

Blaine's phone blared, and he snatched it from the table. "Crosby." He stated as he answered.

"Carter, where have you been?"

Carter explained their ordeal at the field. While they were sifting dirt, a helicopter flew low over their location. So, they hid in the woods while the copter circled. Since they didn't know if they were alone, they turned off their phones for fear of being found. Once the helicopter left, they finished gathering their bullets. And they're en route to the safe house.

I asked, "do you think they knew you were there?"

"We've discussed that, but we have no confirmation. We found no cameras in the area, and that's not to say they didn't hide one somewhere. We should be there in a few minutes."

The call ended, and Blaine exhaled the breath he'd been holding. "Thanks, Celeste, for encouraging me to let it play out."

"Anytime." I paused before adding, "we need to share what we found out too."

"You're right. Then I'll call Jancey and give him your news. He'll need to coordinate with Swank and the DEA, since this involves their investigation."

"There sure are a lot of moving parts to this case. But if it's as big as it seems, it will take everyone working together to make the arrest solid."

Blaine's phone sounded again. His eyebrows drew together as he listened to the caller. He replied, "drive around. I'll have a patrol car help. Where are you?"

Carter gave Blaine his location and then ended the call. Then Blaine called their dispatcher, asking for assistance. They notified Officer Miller of Carter's location. Blaine waited until he received the call from Miller.

"Crosby. Miller. I've spotted a black SUV tailing Carter. How do you want me to handle it?"

Blaine paused. "We need separation. If you want to stop Carter, do it. I'm unsure if conducting a traffic stop on the SUV would be the wisest choice." Miller chuckled as sirens sounded in the background.

Miller relayed, "Carter pulled into a parking lot. The black SUV never stopped. So I'll follow Carter for a while to ensure the SUV is gone."

"Thanks, Miller."

Blaine ran his hands down his face. Then he rubbed his temples. "I feel like I've run a marathon."

"You should have after what you've done today. With Miller on their tail, Carter and Hudson should be here shortly. I'm eager to hear what they found, and then you can share our findings."

We stayed quiet for a while. For me, I wondered when I'd be able to return to work. My exercises were getting more manageable, but the doctor refused to let me put my foot on the floor. There's no way I can be a nurse on crutches. But maybe I could use a knee scooter. I'll ask about that at my doctor's visit in a few days.

Several minutes passed before we heard the garage door lift and then close. We were eager to see the guys. It has been a tense few hours. Hudson entered first. He sported dark circles under his eyes that weren't there before.

"Hudson, has your pain arrived?" I asked, pointing to his shoulder.

"Unfortunately, it has, but we did good." He grinned as he glanced at Carter.

Carter lifted several evidence bags with bullets inside. Then they took turns telling us about their ordeal. They used lasers to triangulate the area they felt Hudson's bullet landed, and they found it. That would be an easy match since it still held blood, presumably from Hudson. Then they recovered a bullet that grazed the officer, but it was deep in a tree trunk.

From that site, they moved to the field. After they had unearthed a bullet, the helicopter arrived, circling their area. They hid amongst the trees until it retreated. Then they set about digging for more bullets. This time they came away with two more bullets, but they suspect more remain in the ground.

Hudson added, "we were halfway here when Carter spotted a tail. Unfortunately, the SUV never got close enough for us to see the occupants or read the tag. That's when we called you. Thanks for sending Miller. We never saw the SUV again."

"Go get cleaned up because we have news to share, too." Hudson and Carter stared at us, but we refused to divulge anything until they showered.

We waited at the table until the men returned. Both had changed clothes, but Hudson had difficulty with his shirt, so he just draped it over his shoulders.

Then, he offered, "after I hear the news, I'm going to nap in one of your spare rooms."

Everyone nodded in agreement because, by his expression, he was in severe pain, and nothing would help but sleep and pain medication. "Hudson, remember you were shot. Pain is expected, but it can be managed. If you need help, I'm here." I offered, and he nodded.

Blaine cued the photos from Casper's file. He thumbed through them so the guys could see them until he reached the one with my shooter's face on it. He highlighted this one. Then both guys looked at me.

"This is the shooter from the field," Carter stated.

"Yes. Here's the photo I took. Now, you tell me. Is it the same man?"

We waited while the duo inspected both pictures. "It's the same man." They agreed with Hudson's statement.

"So, now we know that Casper's file connects our murders to his. Casper and his partner were working on an op with the DEA when someone killed them. I think we can agree who that someone is." Blaine pointed to a guy wearing all black with thick dark hair getting into a black SUV.

"Do we know his name?" Carter asked.

"Not yet. But I hope Captain Swank does." Then Blaine continued with the photo of the barren land and how they wanted to find its location. When Blaine shared my idea, it impressed the men.

Blaine's phone rang. He tapped the speakerphone for Theo. "What's up, Theo? The gang is all here."

Chapter 6

Theo shared his news. "We have two skeletons identified. They were in CODIS after previous arrests. Both American and Caucasian. Someone shot them point blank in an execution-style shooting with a bullet to the forehead."

"Can you give us their names?"

We heard computer keys clicking. Then he rattled off their names. Blaine's eyebrows bunched together, "hold on a minute, Theo." Then Blaine searched on his computer while Carter and I watched because neither of us knew what Blaine was after.

"I thought I recognized those names. Both guys were confidential informants for Casper and his partner. They're listed here as missing over three months ago."

"So, they went missing before Casper was killed. Maybe that's what troubled Casper. Knowing him, he felt responsible for their deaths." I shared.

Theo added, "Your time frame matches mine. We'll handle the notification to the family. Since these two were in the system, I assume the others will be too. At least, it will aid in the process."

The call ended and they stared at each other. Blaine held a pen with paper underneath. "Tell me what we have."

"Bullets from both scenes, and they need a trip to the lab, too. Plus, we have two bodies tied to Casper's file." Carter exclaimed.

"We need to share this with Jancey. Also, when Hudson wakes, we can have him take the bullets to the lab unless you want time away." Blaine looked at Carter, who shrugged his shoulders.

"Only if I can have time for dinner with Alena." Then Carter winked at me. "Let me ask."

He slipped off to speak with Alena in private, leaving me with Blaine. "Why don't you take time away? You've been cooped up with me for days. Everybody needs a change of scenery."

"I'm not leaving you. No discussion." Blaine's comment left no room for questions. So, I didn't bother.

I curled up in an oversized chair, propped my leg on the ottoman, and started a book. Since I had no idea how long I'd be here, I figured I had time to finish it. Besides, that let the guys discuss the case without me hanging around.

Blaine had his phone to his ear, and I assumed he spoke with Jancey. But instead, I heard him mention bullets, the lab, and then the two guys they identified.

Once I heard, I returned to my book. But my mind wandered to Casper and his thoughts about his missing CIs. He took everything personally, so I can only assume he did this, too.

Things turned quiet for a while as Carter and Blaine worked the case. They made calls, added information to their list, and finally leaned back in their chairs. So, did they have a plan?

I grabbed my crutches and worked to slide from the chair. "Can I get you anything, Celeste? That chair looks like it has the best of you." Chuckling, Blaine pointed at the chair.

"This material is not meant for sliding. I'm headed to the coffeepot." I said, grinning.

Blaine offered, "I'll bring it to you. Have you completed your exercises?"

"Not the second set, but I will before bedtime."

Blaine stood from his chair and stretched. Then he poured two cups of coffee. He handed me one. "might as well make two." We clinked cups. Then he went back to the computer. As he sat, his phone rang.

He placed the call on speakerphone so Carter could take part in the conversation. Jancey explained that he'd spoken with Swank, and they'd agreed to a joint task force. Swank requested Celeste stay here since they're still short-staffed. But he agreed to have SWAT stand by if we visited Celeste's house for Casper's files. So the group will meet virtually for an hour. Blaine and Carter will lead the task force, while Harvey will lead it from Swank's department.

When the call ended, Blaine asked me, "do you know Harvey?"

"I've met him a time or two. He's been around forever. Casper described him as analytical."

"Ok. He's leading the task force for Swank's office, and we meet with them virtually tomorrow morning at nine."

Carter checked a text message. "I will have dinner tonight with Alena. So, Hudson can stay here until I return. That way, they'll always be two on guard duty."

I smiled by cringing inwardly. Staying hidden from the world was not something I relished, and I can't stay locked up forever. If it weren't for my leg, I'd be working. And at some point, I must return to work or risk losing my house. Without Casper's income, it will be tough handling the finances. But I'm unsure if I want to stay in that house without Casper, anyway. Maybe this will force me to move and start anew.

Carter left early so he could drop the recovered bullets at the lab. Then he'd have a few hours with Alena. That should reinvigorate him for a while.

After Carter left and with Hudson still asleep, Blaine joined me in the family room. "With all the talk about Casper, I wanted to check on you. How are you holding up?"

"Every day is a little easier. I still think about him, but not as much. But that will change when I return home. I thought earlier about selling the house. It's too much for just me, but then I have nowhere to move."

Blaine tilted his head, "this might sound forward, but I'd like it if you stayed here. Alena mentioned the hospital needed nurses, and then we could see where our relationship goes if you're interested."

"I am interested, just not ready. We've had a spark since I opened my eyes in the hospital and saw you. There's something between us, but I'm holding too much baggage right now to consider bringing you into the mess."

"I'm confident we'll close this case soon, and then we can return to our lives. But I'm sharing that I want you in mine. The rest is up to you." Blaine stated as he leaned over and kissed me.

He left me speechless, so I just gave a slight nod. My mind was cluttered with many questions about a home and a job. Where should I start?

Then I planned to call Alena tomorrow instead of interrupting her date. Maybe she could steer me to the person in charge of hiring at the hospital. But would she keep it a secret? I wasn't ready to let Blaine or Carter know I might move.

Hudson woke starving. He'd slept most of the day, but looked more refreshed than when he started. "Ugh, this shoulder. You were right, Celeste. When the shots wear off, the pain is brutal. Alena gave me some pills, but they put me to sleep."

"Take some Tylenol. It will take the edge away, but you need the reminder that the pain is still there. It will stop you when you try to do something you're not supposed to." I chuckled as I said it.

He grinned, "you know me, huh? Is there any food around here? Where's Carter?"

Blaine added, "yes, there's food. Carter took the bullets to the lab. Then he's having dinner with Alena. He should be home shortly. Then you can go home if you want."

Hudson looked around. "I kind of like it here. Well, let me rephrase that. Let's see the food, and then I'll answer that question."

Motioning for Hudson to follow, Blaine led the way to the kitchen. When he opened the refrigerator and the pantry, Hudson salivated. "This is more food than I have at home, too."

Hudson reached in for a handful of grapes when Blaine's phone sounded. He answered before voice mail. "Carter, what's up?"

Then we waited while Blaine spoke with Carter. Hudson placed his grapes on the table as Blaine discussed Carter's situation, telling him to hold the line.

Blaine looked at Hudson, "Carter is on his way back, but he has a tail, and this time its motorcycles. Two of them. The bikes are racing bikes. He's concerned he'll never outmaneuver them."

Hudson groaned, "he won't. I raced motorcycles in my younger days. The bikes are super speedy. It will take two patrol cars to help Carter escape unless he can lose them at a traffic light."

"Crosby." We heard through the phone. Then a loud noise.

"Carter. Are you okay? Is that wind noise?"

"Yeah." He yelled, "they're right behind me now. I lowered my window in case they started shooting, giving me a chance to return fire."

"Patrol units are headed your way. You've got three minutes to keep them at bay. I've notified dispatch of your situation. You have clearance to use your lights and sirens if you need to."

"Thanks, Crosby. They've split with each bike on the outer edges of the traveling lane. This isn't good." Then tires squealed.

"Carter. Are you still there?" No reply. "Carter? Say something."

Still nothing. Hudson holds his injured shoulder while Blaine paces. Then Hudson asks, "Carter?"

But nothing except noise. They couldn't even tell if the car was still in motion. When suddenly, the tires squealed again. "Carter. Answer me!" Blaine barked.

"Sorry about that. My phone fell onto the floorboard. I stopped one bike by quickly turning into its path. The bike hit my left rear quarter panel, sending the driver airborne. I pulled away once he cleared the car. He was lying in the road last I saw him."

"Okay. Good call. Do you still have the other one on your tail?" Blaine asked, trying to get a picture of what was happening.

"No, not that I can see. A patrol car just passed me, heading to the bike accident. I'm coming your way while I can."

"We'll be waiting," Blaine said, then ended the call.

I glanced at the guys. "that was intense. Carter pulled that scary move. He could have been killed doing that."

No one spoke as they revisited Carter's situation. Instead, they listened to the purr of the garage door as it lifted. Then a car door slammed. Followed by Carter entering the house. "Hey." He said in greeting. "I've got a dented car. Jancey won't be happy."

"But it saved your life, Carter. He'll be fine with it." Blaine offered as he consoled Carter.

Hudson inquired, "did you at least get the bullets to the lab?"

Carter tilted his head. "Yes. I dropped them first."

Then Carter slipped off to his room. He looked shaken, but otherwise okay. I was sleepy, too, now that Carter had returned, so I hobbled to my room to complete my exercises and go to bed. Blaine and Hudson remained at the table.

The loud banging of pots and pans roused me from a deep sleep. I struggled to wake up because I did too many exercises last night. Today, my body will pay for it. Not only did I exercise my leg, but I stretched too.

When I opened the door, the aroma of eggs and bacon had my mouth salivating. "What's going on? Did anything happen?" I asked.

Hudson stood over the stove with one arm in a sling while holding the spatula in the other. "Oh. Good morning, Celeste. Sorry if I woke you. Cooking with one arm isn't easy, but I was hungry, so I made enough for everyone."

"You never mentioned you could cook," I said with an eyebrow lifted.

"I'm not good at it, but when I get hungry, I cook. So if the others would join us, we could all eat together."

The guys emerged from their rooms about that time, rubbing their midsection. "That smells delicious."

Hudson grinned. "We have a meeting this morning, and that calls for nourishment. So, dig in."

Everyone did by piling food onto their plates. Blaine carried mine to the table and then returned to the counter for our coffee. My heart swelled because I didn't know how to handle this without him.

There wasn't much talking during breakfast since we hadn't eaten this well since arriving. Toward the end of the meal, Blaine sipped his coffee, then added, "we need groceries. I'll speak with Jancey about it and see if someone can do it for us. Hudson, are you staying with us?"

He glanced around the table. "I might as well, if you don't mind."

"We'd love to have you." Blaine nodded.

The men carried their dishes to the sink, and I cleaned the kitchen while they prepared for the task force meeting. I heard snippets, but nothing sounded like they had solved the case yet. How much longer would I have to stay here?

Once I cleaned the kitchen, my leg throbbed. I considered the reasons for the delayed healing. It's been weeks since my surgery, and I still have pain. I returned to bed to rest while the men conducted the meeting.

I must have fallen asleep because the men were staring at their computers when I returned to the kitchen. "Hey, Celeste. How was your nap?"

"Good. Have you had your meeting?"

The men chuckled, then Blaine replied, "that was two hours ago."

"Two hours? How could I have slept that long?" I shook my head because I couldn't explain why I always wanted to sleep. It didn't use to be this way.

Blaine described the meeting between their departments and Swanks. Then he said, "Harvey will meet us at your place for Casper's files, but only if you're up for it."

Pausing, I thought about it and decided I'd like to see the house anyway. It might help me with my decision to move. "Sure, set it up."

Blaine faced the guys and grinned. He thought this would help them find the killer and solve Casper's death along with his partner's. Then, dialing the phone, he helped me get to the recliner and raise my leg.

We were traveling to Colorado Springs within thirty minutes, and my inside quivered. How would I feel when these guys started pilfering through my things? That was an uncertainty, but if Casper held a secret file, then we needed it.

We drove in separate cars in case we had to take evasive action. I rode in the backseat of Blaine's car while Hudson rode with Carter. Harvey met us in the driveway. When I exited the vehicle, he said, "Celeste, I am so sorry for your loss. Casper was the best."

"Thanks, Harvey. But Casper said you were the best." Then I grinned, shaking off the sadness overtaking me.

A SWAT truck entered the road and pulled alongside the curb. I glanced at Blaine, and he lifted his shoulders. "Do we need them?" I asked.

"Better safe than sorry. They'll clear the house for us."

When I made it to the door, I saw the marks on the doorframe. I pointed and said, "it might be a good idea. Someone beat us here."

Blaine spoke with the SWAT commander, and they breached the door first. It took five minutes for the group of ten to clear the house. He stood in the doorway. "the house is clear, but someone ransacked it."

I moaned as tears welled up in my eyes. Now, I feared entering my house. What would I find? Blaine stood beside me, and he could feel my tremors. He leaned over and whispered, "I'm here. Come on. We'll do it together."

The SWAT commander stood back as we entered the house. The front room was intact as the kitchen, but the family room and office were in shambles. It shocked me to see things strewn about like they meant nothing. Somehow, these killers suspected Casper of having another file, but how?

I began picking things up from the floor until Blaine stopped me. "You can't do that with your leg? We'll handle it. Let's check out the office first."

Harvey led the way to the office. "Celeste, Casper mentioned keeping paper files. Would you know where he would put them?"

"Over the years, he's used several places. The first is behind the second shelf in the bookcase. Help me over there, and I'll show you." The guys cleared a path for me. I reached up and tapped the corner of the shelf above. A small click sounded, then I pushed slightly on the back, giving way to a hidden compartment. This one was empty.

While I went to the desk, the guys placed the books back on the shelves. While they weren't in any order, it was a friendly gesture. I plopped down in Casper's chair. Then my eyes gravitated to the floor. "Look." I pointed to a pair of knee impressions on the carpet.

Blaine added, "someone's been here. Did they find the files?"

"Let me check." I opened the middle drawer on the left, popping the bottom, which was also empty. "Empty," I said, then I pulled open the bottom right head drawer.

This one took an effort to remove the bottom. Harvey reached down. "let me help, Celeste."

His paws took over the drawer space, so I had no choice but to pull my hands out. I glanced at Blaine just as a car passed the house. Rustling sounded from the front, and the guys trotted to check on the situation.

Blaine returned first, followed by the others. "SWAT prepared for an assault, but the car didn't stop. So it appears it was a neighbor."

I grimaced when I thought about my neighbors. When everyone made it back, I held up a stack of files. Blaine reached for them first. "Let's move to the table."

Everyone left, so I stayed back in the office. I puttered around, trying to put things back in order. There's no way I can leave my house in disarray. But my decision came in the middle of this chaos. I couldn't see myself living here after someone rummaged through my things.

I had no idea what the upstairs looked like, but I couldn't traverse fifteen stairs with this leg. Our bedroom was on the main floor, so I ventured in there. Unfortunately, the killers destroyed our walk-in closet, so I grabbed a few pieces of clothes from the floor, leaving the rest until I returned. Then I grinned when I noticed they had never found the safe.

When I returned to the table, the guys were in deep discussion, with the file contents on top. Some photos held Harvey's attention. Then I heard, "I can't believe it."

"What can't you believe, Harvey? Is that not what we needed?"

"It is what we needed, but what I found shocked me." He gave me a look of disbelief.

"Can you share what you found?" I asked, curious.

"This." He handed me a picture. I studied it, trying to understand the issue.

"Isn't this Officer Davis? Who is he shaking hands with?" I asked.

"That's what I need to know. Office Davis has been with the department for years, and people have wondered how he affords many toys. I think I just answered that question. The guy in the picture with him is our prime suspect in your husband's death."

The picture flitted to the table. I didn't want to hold it. "Then bring Davis in for questioning. Let's find out what he knows." I said in a terse tone.

Blaine rubbed my arm when he heard my tone. He knew this upset me. Harvey suggested he meet with Swank first. Then he'd share with the task force. "Share what?"

When the voice sounded, everyone cringed. Swank stood at the entry. "Hey Celeste, you knew I'd be here."

He walked over to me and wrapped me in a hug. It felt so good to be with this man. Captain Swank was like a father to Casper and me.

After our greeting, he stared at Harvey. "Well, show me."

The situation made Harvey uncomfortable when he showed Swank the picture of Officer Davis shaking hands with a wanted man. Swank glanced at the picture, then at Harvey. "Why is Davis shaking hands with that man?"

"That's what we want to know, sir," Harvey said.

Swank keyed his radio, then requested Davis to meet him at his office in an hour. "I'll find out." He turned, leaving without a word. Instead, he huffed and puffed his way out the front door.

We stood at the table, wondering about our next step. Then Harvey suggested he return to the station while the guys get back to safety.

I looked around the house, knowing I'd have tons of work. As I locked it, a lone tear escaped as it ran down my cheek. I took a deep breath before facing the group. Blaine's eyes bore into mine as he understood my pain.

The return trip to the safe house was quiet. Neither Blane nor I spoke much because I had too many things running through my mind. Blaine talked with Carter and Hudson over their cell phones, but I heard little of their conversation. As Blaine helped me into the house, he took a call from Jancey.

I wandered off to my bedroom for some alone time while Blaine dealt with Jancey and the guys. Jancey questioned how an officer could turn against his oath, but no one offered an answer. So, Blaine tried to turn the conversation to Officer Davis' meeting with Captain Swank. Jancey admitted to hearing nothing. Why hasn't he called?

After exercising and taking a shower, I joined the guys at the table. They sat in the same chairs as when I left. "Anything new?" I prodded.

"Nothing. Not one word. It's been two hours. Officer Davis should have shown by now." Blaine leaned over the table, resting his elbows while rubbing his neck. I noticed worry lines etched on his forehead. Those weren't there earlier. This case is wearing on these guys. They've worked this one inside a safe house instead of on the street. That's nothing short of miraculous.

I propped against the counter so I could reach the coffee cups. After I poured a cup, I stayed there because I didn't want to interrupt. When Blaine's phone sounded, everyone flinched.

"Jancey, we are all here. What have you heard?"

"It's not what you want to hear. Swank called. His officer came to the meeting, but he bolted when Swank showed him the picture of him shaking hands with a murder suspect."

"What do you mean, he bolted?" Hudson asked.

"He fled the building, and no one can find him. This is a captain's worse fear of having one of your own officers turn against the oath they take and jump to the criminal side. Swank confided that he should have seen it earlier. Davis has all the toys a man could ever want, and he should have investigated it." Jancey explained with a tinge of sadness. It's obvious he feels sorry for Swank.

Carter ran his hand down his face. "did Swank get the guy's name?"

"No, Carter, he didn't. The time he showed Davis the picture, he fled. So while they search for Davis, let's continue our path. Have you heard from Theo lately? I was hoping for more identifications on the murder victims?"

"I haven't heard from Theo, but I'll follow up today. We have a few leads to follow from Casper's files. Let's talk later."

The call ended, and all the guys just stared out the window. Their one viable lead is in the wind. Blaine was unsure what leads he referred to, but he couldn't talk to his captain any longer. He needed time to think.

As minutes ticked by, my nerves got the better of me. We still have no name for the murder suspect. Officer Davis fled, and we were out of leads. So, where does that leave me? I was tired of staying locked away.

"Can you use me as bait?" All heads swiveled in my direction. Their eyes were wide as saucers, and I couldn't help but snicker.

Blaine spoke first, "absolutely not. These guys could kill anyone of us from a rooftop. There's another way. We just haven't found it yet."

A text message alert dinged, and everyone checked their phones. Blaine grinned. "Theo identified another skeleton."

Blaine dialed for Theo, and they chatted until Blaine asked about his identity. Theo recited the victim's name, and Blaine paused. He rechecked Casper's file and another match.

After ending the call, Blaine said, "these folks are killing Swank's CIs. I think Casper was on to Officer Davis, but the CIs were already dead before he picked up on the connection. Davis provided this murder suspect the list of CIs his department uses."

"Could our CIs be in jeopardy?" Carter inquired.

Then I asked, "why would someone target a CI? They can only share what little information they have, right?"

"Most CIs are drug dealers. That's how they become a CI. We drop charges as long as they give us inside information in return. It's a win for both. What makes little sense is why they're killing the CIs. Were they mixed up in their drug business?"

Hudson shared, "it makes perfect sense if the department was using the CIs to gather intel on our suspect."

The group nodded. Hudson's statement said it all.

"We need to determine if all the CIs are dead. Then I'll call Swank and deliver more bad news."

Blaine stepped to my side as I studied the faces of the guys sworn to protect me. Then, he walked over and rubbed my arms as he said, "just a little more time, and we'll have him. We're getting closer."

I nodded because it scared me to speak for fear of crying, and I promised myself I wouldn't do that anymore. Crying accomplishes nothing. Blaine poured a cup of coffee and returned to the table.

He dialed Captain Swank. They discussed Davis, then Blaine delivered the news about the deaths of his CIs. That was too much. The news enraged him as he put two and two together. Davis provided his criminal friends with the list and put a hit on Casper and his partner.

When Blaine's call ended, he looked at the group sitting around the table. Then he said, "that must be the hardest thing ever. Working with someone day in and day out, and then they turn on you."

Hudson and Carter shook their heads. "I've never understood that move. Davis has been around the department for decades. Why throw that away for a few toys?" Carter asked while staring at his hands.

He never got his answer because Blaine's phone interrupted their conversation. So he tapped the speakerphone when he saw Jancey's number on the caller ID.

"Jancey. We're here. What's up?"

"Get to the truck stop. There's been a murder."

Blaine looked at me, and I nodded. "Go with Carter. Hudson is here."

Carter stood as Blaine grabbed his keys and his phone. Blaine winked at me as they trotted out the door. Then Hudson tensed now that he was in charge of my safety.

I dove into my book as Hudson paced. He circled the house, checking each window and door as he passed.

"Hudson, take a break. You're tiring me out with your pacing. We're fine." I suggested.

He shook his head as he said, "there's no way I could look Blaine in the eye if something happened to you on my watch."

"No one knows we're here, Hudson." He didn't reply as he walked down the hallway to double-check the windows and doors.

An hour passed without a call from Blaine and Carter. While I grew more concerned by the minute, I couldn't share with Hudson. He held enough worry for us both. Then, finally, Hudson's phone sounded.

He placed it on the end table between the sofa and the recliner so I could hear Blaine. "Blaine, we're here."

"It's another CI. This guy had his wallet in his pocket, and we gleaned his name from his driver's license. Hazel is with me and she remembered this guy coming in for food. After he finished, she had just refilled his tea glass when another man joined him. They left together. She thinks it was two or three hours ago."

"Can we check the videos?" Hudson asked.

"Carter is on that now. Theo just arrived. Once he finishes, we'll return to the house. Do either of you need anything while we're out?" Blaine asked.

"I don't," I replied, and Hudson concurred.

"Okay. I need to run. Theo is waving for me." He ended the call, and I wondered what Theo found.

Now that we knew they were safe, Hudson settled. Instead of continuously monitoring the door and window locks, he did it at fifteen-minute intervals. Finally, he stood at the front window for a few minutes, staring at something.

Finally, my curiosity won. "What's happening out there? You've been in the same place for a while."

"There's a work truck parked across the street. I've seen no one exit the truck."

"Is there a logo on it?" I asked.

"A plumber's logo, but I can't read the company's name from this angle. Oh, there they are. Two men walked to the van's rear. They're rolling an enormous piece of equipment to the door. Maybe they're legit." Hudson described, but he didn't move. Instead, he stared out that window until the workers left.

Hudson's phone rang, but he couldn't remember where he had left it. "It's on the table, Hudson."

He trotted to it, tapping the green button before voicemail answered. Blaine spoke in a clipped tone. "Pack your things and leave quickly. I'll explain later. Carter's keys are on the table beside the computer."

Hudson looked at me, and I moaned. Then, instead of waiting for me to hobble to my room, Hudson picked me up with one arm and placed me on the bed. "Get your things. I'll pack everything else."

I threw things in a bag, not waiting to fold anything. Then placed the bag over my head, so I could carry it and use the crutches simultaneously. Hudson entered the kitchen from the garage just as I walked into the kitchen. "Did you get the guy's clothes? And what about the computers?"

He nodded, "Everything is in the car. Let's go."

Once we settled into Carter's car, he looked at me, "I don't have a clue what we'll face out there." Hudson pointed over his shoulder to ensure I understood what he referred to like I didn't know. "But just hang on. Blaine will call us back with a plan."

Chapter 7

Hudson drove the car one-handed, and he did it with precision. His head swiveled, with one eye on the rearview mirror. "Anyone following us?" I asked.

"Not yet." He said in a clipped tone as he glanced at his phone sitting upright in the console. It concerned him that Blaine hadn't called yet. Without the call, it left them with an uncertain path.

We sat at a traffic light when Blaine called. I pressed the speakerphone button, and Hudson answered the call. "What's going on, Blaine? Where should we go?"

"That's what we're working on. We have credible evidence of a bomb threat. It mentioned the word house. We were unsure if it meant the safe house, so we sent you packing out of precaution. Jancey should call shortly with a new place for us. Were you able to get all our belongings?"

"Yes, clothes and computers are in the trunk. Don't yell when you see the clothes. We hope there's an iron at the next stop." They chuckled because no one took the time to fold their clothes.

There was a pause, and we waited. "I'll text you your next address. It's not too far from the last house. We're headed there too, and we'll have the keys." Blaine ended the call as he spoke to someone.

Ten seconds passed before Hudson's phone dinged with an address. Hudson moaned when he saw it. "What's wrong with the address?" I questioned.

"The homes in that area are huge. It will be harder to secure, but we'll make it work. At least I have something to do in my downtime." Hudson glanced at me and smiled. That's when I noticed all these guys could be brothers. They're stocky, tall, and have soft eyes but piercing when trouble strikes.

Alena popped into my mind, and while I wanted to speak with her about a job, I couldn't do it in front of Hudson. He would definitely tell Blaine, and I don't want that to happen. So I made a mental note to find a quiet place later so we could speak freely.

We entered another subdivision, and Hudson was right. These homes are massive. "How did this house become a safe house for the department?" I asked.

"We seized it in a raid a few years back. I'm surprised the department still maintains it."

Hudson made a right, then a left, followed by another left. We entered the drive and followed it to the garage. There was a circular drive that connected to this drive, too. The house was a combination of stone and siding with an oversized front door.

Blaine and Carter pulled in behind us just as we exited the car. "The garage door openers are on the kitchen counter. We'll get those and pull our cars inside. No need to alert anyone to our presence." Blaine instructed.

Once inside, I questioned Blaine, "Tell me about this bomb threat."

"The body found at the truck stop was also a CI. He had a wadded piece of paper in his pocket with the words house, C4, and is. Unfortunately, we never found the missing portion of the note. The word on the note is confusing because we're uncertain if that's the word or if it means Davis. While we don't have an address, we didn't want to chance the bomb being at the safe house."

"We appreciate that. Why would they resort to a bomb when they've used guns in the past?"

I received a shoulder shrug, then Blaine added, "Maybe they're tired of killing one at a time. If they position the bomb to gather the most bodies, they will take all four of us out with one bomb."

Shivers crept up my spine as I wished I hadn't asked that question. "But then they'd bring more attention to themselves, right?"

"I suppose, but I'm unsure if that matters anymore." Blaine didn't elaborate, and I didn't push. Some things are better left unsaid.

Carter called the group to the table. "Here's the truck stop video from inside the restaurant." He played it, and we watched the victim enter. Then Hazel showed him to a table. He was enjoying a meal when another guy sat across from him in the booth. They spoke briefly. Blaine noted the time on the video as they left the screen. "Hold on. Do we have the video from outside?"

Nodding, Carter pressed a few keys. Then the video began. The new guy followed the victim outside, and their arms appeared every so often. They spoke off-screen, but the victim fell to the ground away from the camera as his feet came into view.

I mumbled, "I wish these guys would remove their sunglasses, so we'd have a decent visual."

Carter replied, "me too. That would make it easier. Did Casper mention a name in his file other than the CI list?"

"I'm unsure if he had one. From the outside, it looks like they were using their CIs to help infiltrate the drug business. I can only assume Davis found out what was happening, and he turned on the CIs and detectives. If he had kept his mouth shut, the likelihood of this happening would have been negligible." Blaine explained as he jotted a note on his pad.

Theo called, and Blaine tapped the speakerphone. "Theo. The group is all here. I hope this is a good call."

"Hello, all. I'm working on the murder victim from the truck stop. I found two fibers on his arm that don't belong to him. Blaine and Carter, I need to see the clothes you wore to the scene. I've ruled out the officer. Send me texts with pictures. If I need a sample, I'll let you know. Also, this guy had dirt on his shoes that wasn't local. I'm still working on that. That's all I have."

"Theo, can you share more about the soil? What type is it?" Carter asked.

"I can't answer that yet. I'm running tests now. All I can say is it held more sand than normal for our area."

All heads bobbed. So, what does that mean? Where is there sandy soil around here? Blaine ended Theo's call with more questions than answers.

"Why would our victim have sandy soil on his shoes? Is there sand in the soil at the truck stop?"

No one responded because no one knew. "I'll ask Theo to sample the soil at the truck stop for comparison."

Carter had his face turned to this computer. "what about landscapers? They mix sand with dirt for vegetation growth. The article doesn't specify if the entire state does this, or if our victim's shoes held the same type of sand."

Blaine wrote more notes on his pad. "The victim must have driven from the place with the sand to the truck stop. But I can't see the sand staying in place for long."

"Did we find his car?" Hudson asked. Blaine looked at Carter for an answer.

"No. We ran his driver's license, but the car registered to him wasn't in the lot. So we asked an officer to check his apartment. No one knows how he arrived." Blaine explained.

Carter added, "we spoke with the patrons too, hoping they saw the guy arrive in a car. Hazel promised to inform us if a car remained in the lot tonight. So we'd assume that would be his."

I held Casper's file in front of me as I revisited it. If anyone can read between the lines, it should be me. Using pen and paper, I drew a timeline. This investigation began seventeen months ago. They monitored a few drug buys the first few months, but nothing out of the ordinary. Then, eleven months ago, the dynamics shifted. Casper and his partner started jotting notes in some sort of shorthand. The strange thing is that there are no names mentioned. The players are numbered. But where is the guide for the players? There must be one somewhere.

While I perused the file, the guys worked on the soil. First, they studied a map of Colorado, searching for a sandy region. When they found none, they turned to satellite imagery of the state. They separated the form into sections, finding a few areas of concern.

I listened to them discuss their areas as I continued studying the file. It disheartened me when I came up empty-handed on the list of players. How could Casper remember the numbers associated with so many folks? He wrote it down somewhere, but where?

"Did anyone find a list of names associated with a number? I've searched Casper's file and didn't find it." I asked.

"Not that I recall. Why would you want that?"

"Casper wrote notes in shorthand. He gave the players a number instead of using their names. If we had that sheet, we'd have a name." I smiled as I explained my find.

"Celeste, you're brilliant." All eyes turned to Blaine, and a slight blush crept upward from his neck. Everyone laughed. "Where would Casper keep the list?"

I shrugged my shoulders because I hadn't a clue. The list wasn't in the file, which makes sense if you're striving to keep the names a secret. But it must be somewhere readily accessible. "Did the department keep Casper's phone? He typed on that thing all the time. Maybe that's where it is."

Blaine grabbed his phone and hit the speed dial button for Detective Harvey. When he answered, Blaine explained his call. Blaine whispered with his hand covering the mouthpiece, "he's checking the logbook for Casper's phone."

"It's at the lab. I'll run over there and get it. When I have it, what am I looking for?"

There was a slight hesitation as Blaine wondered how much information to share, but since he had no choice, he explained what they were after. He promised to call when he had it in his hands.

Hudson shared, "if the list is on the phone, it will be a major step to closure. Has Casper used his shorthand before, in cases?"

"I've seen notes in shorthand ever since we married. It was his way of giving me plausible deniability. I never pushed for information on his cases for fear I'd jeopardize them."

"Look what I found on the satellite maps." Hudson pointed to his computer. The guys gathered around him while I stayed seated. They'd share when they could.

"Is that a crop of something?" Carter asked.

Everyone looked to Hudson. "That's what it appears. But look at what's beside the crop."

Hudson clicked the map and then slid it over, showing a perfect circle cut into the tree line.

"Whoa, Hudson, that might be our helicopter landing pad. How far is this area from the field?" Blaine asked.

"5.3 miles by foot, but with an ATV, you could go off-road and cut that in half." Hudson grinned as he relished in the information.

"Do you have the coordinates? I'd like to run this by Jancey. Maybe SWAT could check it out for us."

"Sure thing, Blaine." Then Hudson recited the coordinates just as Blaine's phone sounded.

"Harvey," Blaine answered as he tapped the FaceTime button, wondering why he used FaceTime on this call.

He held the phone in his large hand, showing it to us. "Here's the phone. The lab hasn't hacked it yet. Celeste, do you know Casper's password to enter the phone?"

I rattled off a string of numbers. They stared at me, trying to figure out what it meant. Of course, I wasn't sharing that.

Harvey entered the information and his eyebrows bunched. "That didn't work. Does he have another password?"

I sat up in my chair. "It didn't work," I mumbled. Then I asked, "Harvey, can you hold the phone up to your screen and show me the bottom?"

Everyone stared at me, but I knew what I was doing. Harvey did as I instructed, but I asked him to tilt it slightly. "That's not Casper's phone," I stated with intensity. "I don't know who that phone belongs to, but it's not Casper's. Since our phones matched, I dabbed a spot of blue nail polish on his phone, while mine has red." I raised my phone to prove my point.

Harvey was speechless. He didn't know where to go from here. "Whose phone is this, then?"

"Check Casper's partner's log for a phone. Maybe they switched them." Hudson suggested.

Harvey ended the call without so much as a goodbye. I glanced at the guys, wondering what had happened when Casper died. No one told me the story. But did I want to know the details?

While the group pondered the cellphone snafu, Theo called. "I won't need your clothes for fiber testing. The fiber found on the victim's arm was a type of thin cotton with a design in the weave. The color was light blue, or some call it baby blue. Unfortunately, our victim wore nothing that matched that color. So, either the killer had it on, or someone else was on the scene."

"Thanks for the update. Anything on the soil?"

"I'm still working on it, but the sample is so small, it's taking more time," Theo explained.

"Let us know when you can."

The call ended, and Carter suggested, "I'll watch the truck stop videos again and see if anyone wore something with light blue material."

We nodded at Carter. At least he had a plan. The rest of us stared at the others. Casper's cell phone bugged me more than anything. That might be the answer. If it's not in police custody, where is it?

The guy's phone beeped with an alert, and the noise startled me. Then read the alert, then moaned. "Swank placed a statewide BOLO for Officer Davis and listed him as armed and dangerous," Blaine explained.

"Could Davis have taken Casper's phone?" I asked. "He worked with him, but I don't recall who the responding officer was to Casper's scene."

Pens flew across the paper as the guys entered the note on their pads. That was something else to follow. If Davis responded, there's a high probability he has Casper's phone. That means we'll solve this case another way.

"Who has access to Casper's computer at work? I can't imagine the only CI list being on the phone. He wouldn't depend solely on the phone for storing just valuable information." So I stated, trying to find a way to that report.

Jancey called the group, and they shared their information with him. He couldn't explain the phone mishap either, but requested an update once they resolved it. Then he offered to call Swank for the computer information, since their IT unit would have to decrypt the files on Casper's computer. Blaine shared Theo's update on the light blue fiber, but nothing new on the soil sample.

Then Jancey gave the real reason for his call. "Celeste and Hudson, you escaped the bomb at the safe house. The bomb squad found it tucked under the back deck at the kitchen wall. They set it to detonate last night."

I shared a glance at Hudson and nodded. Then I winked at Blaine as he asked, "any other warnings we should prepare for? Since arriving, we've not left here, so they shouldn't have our location."

Jancey replied, "I can only hope." Then we heard a dial tone.

"I forgot to mention the crops," Blaine said to himself as he tapped Jancey's contact card. When he answered, Blaine explained Hudson's discovery. Jancey agreed they needed to check it out, since the other place never panned out, and they watched the building for days without activity.

Blaine recited the coordinates, and Jancey offered SWAT to look at it since they had off-road vehicles. Then he'd report the findings.

Harvey called, and Blaine answered for the group. "There's no other cellphone in evidence for Casper or his partner. I hate to be the one to say this, but it appears Officer Davis made a swap. He was first on the scene of the shooting. Swank fears the phone in evidence is a burner phone, and Davis commandeered Casper's phone and his partners. There's no other feasible explanation."

"Thanks for sharing. Do you know if Davis was alone when he responded?"

"Hold the line. I'll check." We heard Harvey work on the computer keys. "Based on the report, Davis was first on scene within ninety seconds of the shooting. Then two other patrol cars arrived within three minutes of the call. The time difference gave Davis plenty of time to do whatever he needed."

I stammered, "Davis knew the shooting would take place at that time and location." This man makes my blood boil. I wanted to track him down myself.

The guys turned my way, but they saw nothing but rage. I would take my last breath on earth, tracking that man down and seeing him rot in prison. How could he turn on another cop? That is despicable. Blaine continued staring while the other returned to

Harvey's call. Finally, the call ended, and Blaine joined me on the sofa.

"I can see the anger on your face. We'll find Davis. There's a nationwide manhunt for him now. Those of us good cops don't like the few bad ones that tarnish the badge, so every cop out there has his picture. Transportation hubs are on the lookout too."

While I listened to Blaine, that meant nothing. "Davis has other means of transportation. He won't be traveling by commercial planes, trains, or boats. He has other means now that he is involved with the drug cartel. With all the drug leader provides him, they owe Davis. He has a ride out of the US waiting if he hasn't already taken it." I fumed.

No one had a reply because they knew I was right. Davis wouldn't sit around waiting for a fellow officer to arrest him. So Blaine fired off a text alerting Jancey to the chance Davis would fly from a private airfield. That would make it almost impossible to find Davis.

Blaine swore to himself that he'd find Davis and charge him appropriately. Davis won't get away with what he's done. Blaine started to the coffee pot when he heard a crash. He turned, finding me on the floor, sobbing, holding my leg.

"Celeste, what happened?" He asked as he trotted to my side. The other guys watched the exchange.

"I forgot about my leg. Pain soared up my leg when I put my weight on it, then it crumbled. Then I followed. Sorry guys." It embarrassed me I caused such a scene as I struggled back to the chair. But that was a learning moment, too. Not to let rage win. Instead, focus on my recovery. Once I recover, I can use the rage to track Davis down and make him pay for what he's done.

"Let me help you." Blaine placed his arms under mine and raised me from the floor. My eyes watered with the movement.

"I'm heading to my room. After that fall, I need to check my incision. Plus, today, I'm supposed to check in with my boss. She'll eventually tire of hearing my same excuses for not returning to work." I couldn't meet Blaine's eyes for fear of shedding more tears.

We walked into the bedroom, and he helped me lie down. He lifted my pants leg and grimaced. Then I looked. "How stupid could I be? Now it's bleeding again."

Blaine's eyebrows drew together as he said, "I would've thought the incision would have healed by now. So it shouldn't be bleeding."

"The surgeon explained the stitches on the outside will be the last to heal since I have so many stitches inside. So this blood might come from an inside stitch. I'll see if I can stop it." I applied a pressure pack to the incision and laid my head back. Then I glanced at Blaine.

Our eyes met. I saw sadness in his eyes. Then a sparkle passed over them. Carter broke up at our moment. "Blaine. We need you." He squeezed my hand before leaving.

As I contemplated my life, I heard the guys talk, but from my distance, it was nothing more than a mumble. My mind kept wandering back to Casper and his list of players. Where would he keep the list? I recalled our house and what Casper did over the last few months of his life. Could he have stored it somewhere in the house? He never mentioned a safe to me if he did, which would've been strange. The gym!

"Blaine. Come see me when you have a chance." Before I finished, he came rushing through the door.

"What's wrong?"

"Casper and I have a gym membership. The gym has lockers. Do you think Casper placed the list in his locker?" I asked with a head tilt and an eyebrow raised.

"It's worth checking out. Actually, anywhere you think Casper could hide a list, we need to hear it. So we can check on it."

"I want to go. It'll be easier with me there since I have the code to the lock." I smiled.

"Let's see your leg." Blaine lifted the pressure pack and shrugged his shoulder. "It might have clotted. But I'm unsure what to expect with exertion."

I nodded as I looked at the incision, too. I've seen worse in my profession, but this wasn't the best it's looked, either. "Once I clean it, we'll decide." I reached for my crutches with one foot on the floor before swinging the other down. Blaine watched me hobble into the bathroom.

When he left, I turned on the water and cleaned my leg. But before returning to the guys, I dialed Alena. She answered on the first right. We chatted at first, then she asked about my leg. When I told her how stupid I'd been, she immediately suggested a doctor see me. I put her off when I explained the list. Then I shared the reason for my call. It exhilarated her to hear of my interest in a nursing position at her hospital. After that, she promised not to say a word to the guys until I decided on my next step.

After the call, I wandered out to join the guys. They were in deep thought as I cleared the doorway. "What's wrong?" I asked in a concerned tone.

"We're waiting for SWAT to check on the crops. That's the only thing that explains the sandy soil on our victim's shoes. We read where landscapers add sand to the soil for drainage, since most of the Colorado soil is dense." Blaine explained.

"Why would the victim be near the crops? That seems odd." I questioned.

Hudson replied, "he might have found the crops. Then decided to surveil them. But I can't answer why the victim met his killer. Did he not know this guy was the killer?"

Everyone glanced around the room, but there were no answers. Instead, Blaine's phone rang, and he tapped the button for the speaker just as he answered. Jancey spoke loud enough for everyone to hear. "The SWAT commander stated that there are fresh footprints on the ground on the outer edge of the plot. The crop is so new they couldn't tell us what is being grown, but they pulled some, and we have the lab test them. It took them a while to circle the field because of its size, and when they did, they found the circles. They are definitely helicopter landing pads, and their photos will prove it. Now, they're tracking vehicle tracks from one of the landing pads."

Jancey ended the call once he'd given us the information. But I saw nothing to do with it. We have a crop of some kind, landing pads, and vehicle tracks. I didn't foresee the SWAT members tracking the vehicle if they were as deep in the forest as I believe.

My mind returned to Casper's list, but my ringing phone broke my concentration. When I answered, I inhaled deeply. I listened as the gym's receptionist explained we hadn't paid for our upcoming quarter. Then she offered her condolences for Casper's death. I explained about my injury, but somehow I needed to keep Casper's locker locked until I could get there.

Blaine heard my conversation, then he spoke to the guys. They agreed we needed to check out, too. "Celeste, ask her to hold it until we get there tomorrow."

I tilted my head at Blaine's request and asked the receptionist, and she agreed. However, the thought of opening Casper's locker had me concerned. It still held some of his clothes, which would carry his scent. Could I keep it together in front of this group? All I could do was try. If we're going to Colorado Springs tomorrow, maybe they'd let us swing by the house again.

Later in the day, we'd heard nothing from SWAT on the vehicle tracks. We assumed they were a bust. All I thought of was Casper's locker and if I could open it without causing another scene.

Blaine checked in with Theo again, but the soil sample was so small that without a comparison, he couldn't do anything with it. After sharing about the crop field, Theo asked for a soil sample. He'd compare the two for us, confirming one of the last places our victim would have been before his death.

Before ending the call, Blaine asked Theo if he'd received a small plant to test. Blaine looked at the group when he said no, ending the call. "So, what do you make of that? SWAT hasn't dropped off the plant to Theo yet."

"That is odd. It's been hours since they were in the field. Where are they?" Carter asked.

"Call Jancey, Blaine. Make sure he's heard from SWAT."

Blaine tapped Jancey's number, and it went straight to voicemail. He left a brief message with all sorts of things running through his mind.

It was after supper before Jancey returned the call, stunning the crowd. The group listened as Jancey explained the SWAT team was missing. Not one member, but the entire team. The team traveled in the SWAT truck, which is also missing. We've had no radio contact from any of the eight members and nothing since they followed the vehicle tracks some two miles from the crop field.

Jancey's information left us speechless. He continued by adding the FBI has joined the search for the SWAT members as this is unprecedented territory for this department. Then Jancey asked us the dreaded question.

"Do you suspect any of the SWAT members to be involved with Davis?" Everyone stayed silent. Then heads started shaking from side to side.

Blaine answered, "I can't say for sure because I never suspected Davis." Then the others repeated Blaine's statement. The guys were in a predicament because this left them wondering who to trust.

When the call ended, silence remained. Each guy looked at the others, considering their involvement. Finally, Blaine stated, "if any of you are involved in this mess with Davis, come clean, now." Unfortunately, his tone left little meaning.

Again, silence until Carter asked, "What about you, Blaine? Are you involved with Davis?"

I inhaled because I'd witnessed none of the guys speak to Blaine like that. But they had a right. They needed to know their leader wasn't on the take too.

"No, I'm not, but I'm guessing one of the SWAT team members is working with Davis. Do either of you know the SWAT guys?"

"I know them when I see them, but most came out of Denver when we started our SWAT team. They were on a team over there, and when their captain retired, they wanted to stay together."

Blaine thought through Carter's explanation. Then he asked, "has anyone recently joined the team?"

Hudson replied, "Officer Porter joined about six months ago, but I think he ended up on Team B. Team A is missing, right? Porter tried to get me to try out for sniper, but I never got around to it."

I mumbled, "it's a good thing you didn't because we'd be looking for you." Then, turning the page in my book, I felt eyes on me. I looked up, and everyone stared back at me. "What? It's true."

Then everyone laughed. Hudson added, "thanks for putting things in perspective for me, Celeste."

I nodded and gave a half wave. Carter pointed to his computer as he said, "here's the area map. If the SWAT team left the police department, I surmise they'd take this road. It leads directly to the area of concern. Then they would hike into the crop field from here."

"You're suggesting someone knew their route."

"Yes, Blaine, I am. That's the only way the suspects knew where to find them."

Blaine studied the computer by zooming in and out a few times before he felt comfortable with the information. Then, he tapped Jancey's number and waited.

Everyone listened in on the conversation. Blaine didn't hold back on his thoughts concerning a rogue SWAT member. It left Jancey speechless. After two hellos, Jancey returned to the line, saying he couldn't believe there would be another lousy cop out there, but he understood our dilemma. He promised to look into it.

Hudson asked, "what about a couple of us going to the field? So we can take soil samples and grab a plant for Theo. Especially since they have no idea where we're staying."

Carter looked to Blaine but with uncertainty in his eyes. "We're staying put until we hear something from Jancey. But we'll have to chance it if the SWAT team doesn't come forth. Without the soil samples, we have no way of connecting our last victim to the field." Blaine explained.

"What about the list of players? We never found it." I asked. "Should we attempt another visit to my house? It's there, but I'm unsure where Casper stored it."

"Then we have the gym. What about the locker? Should we check there too?" Carter questioned.

There were so many variables to consider that he didn't know which way to turn first. The gym would be the safest because of all the people, but there was still the drive over there. Would the killers expect us as the gym?

Jancey called, and Blaine tapped the speakerphone. "Officer Porter is new to SWAT. He's assigned to Team B, but they had a guy out, so he filled in. Officer Porter and Officer Davis were partners for a while about five years ago."

"Unbelievable." Blaine fumed.

"Maybe Porter knows where Davis is hiding," Carter suggested.

Jancey made it perfectly clear to call in favors. They need the SWAT team returned unharmed. He ended the call in a huff.

Blaine added, "where would you hide a SWAT vehicle full of men?"

"That's a good question. Are there any caves around the field?" I asked.

Then Hudson chuckled, "another good question. But I wouldn't know about caves large enough to hide the SWAT truck. I would think a garage would be easier."

Blaine returned to the computer as he searched for places to hide a large vehicle. Nothing showed promise. He stood, ran his fingers through his hair, and then walked to the coffee pot.

My phone blared, jarring us from our thoughts. I answered and cringed. When the call ended, I shared. "I have a doctor's appointment at the hospital tomorrow morning at ten."

The guys shared a glance, knowing they couldn't stay hidden forever. Nodding, Blaine looked over his shoulder, "we'll all go with two in each car. Then on the return trip, we'll trade cars. Maybe we'd have time to stop at the gym too. That would be less place to search."

I hopped to my room for my late day exercises. The thought of visiting the doctors had my nerves acting. Since I could barely touch the incision, I definitely didn't want someone else to. Then the idea of physical therapy found its way into my mind, and I shuddered. Is my leg ever going to feel right again? My profession requires me to be on my feet for an eight- or twelve-hour shift. What will I do if I can't be a nurse? I've wanted to be a nurse since I was a youngster. and life would never be the same without it.

The rest of the day was quiet. There had been no news on the SWAT vehicle. So, the team had been missing for eight hours, and things looked rough for them when I wandered off to bed. But in the overnight hours, I awoke to the guys talking, and their energy level was off the charts.

I couldn't pull myself out of bed, so I called for Blaine. When he entered the room, he apologized for waking me. "What's the excitement about?"

"The SWAT Team members are safe. They could finally free themselves from their bindings. Officer Porter commandeered the vehicle, forcing them to drive to a secluded area outside town. Porter bound and gagged each member, leaving them in the truck. Once they freed themselves, they called Jancey, and he called me. Now, Porter and Davis are wanted by the FBI."

"That's fantastic. Was anyone hurt?" I asked.

"No, other than a few burn marks. Porter caught the guys by surprise by using their tasers. As the members were incapacitated, he tied and gagged them. Get some sleep. See you in the morning."

Blaine slipped through the doorway, and I closed my eyes, returning to my dreams. Finally, after the overnight news, morning arrived quickly. My anxiety level was through the roof because I didn't want to visit the doctor. But I also knew there was no way out of it too.

After I completed my exercises and showered, I was ready for the day. The guys stood when I hopped into the kitchen. Carter and Hudson slipped off, leaving me with Blaine. He prepared my coffee and brought me some oatmeal. We'd only been together for a few weeks, and he knew what I liked and catered to that fact.

Then I remembered my conversation with Alena. She hadn't called me either, which concerned me, but maybe I'd get to see her today. Blaine asked, "what's wrong, Celeste? You look preoccupied this morning?"

"I guess I am, in a way. This doctor's visit concerns me. I should be able to use my leg by now, but the pain is so great. What will I do if I can't be a nurse?"

"Come on now. Don't think like that. Let's hear what the doctor says first. Then we take it one step at a time." Blaine said as he rubbed my forearm.

"I shouldn't ask this, but you will go into the doctor's office with me."

"Of course I will." He leaned over and peeked me on the cheek. I felt redness take over my neck and face, but Blaine never mentioned it.

Blaine drove me while Carter drove Hudson. We left the house in tandem and headed to the hospital. The guys changed lanes and took different roads, but they ended back together as we entered the parking lot. They parked beside each other, throwing the police decal on the dash.

Blaine helped me into the doctor's office on the back side of the emergency room. Carter and Hudson stayed outside, inhaling the fresh air. When the nurse escorted us to a room, Blaine helped me onto the examination table and lifted my pants leg before sitting in a corner chair.

The doctor came in and stammered when he saw Blaine. I confirmed I asked Blaine to be here, so the doctor agreed. The doctor questioned the incision, but he moved on from it when he announced he needed a CT scan of the incision. That's when I knew what he was after, and I moaned my displeasure.

Chapter 8

Blaine stared at me because he didn't understand. So, I explained the CT scan. "There's a possibility I have a blood clot in my leg. That's the reason for my intense pain."

The doctor's eyes met mine. "Are you the nurse looking for a job here?"

Before I could answer, Blaine said, "I hope so." Then he winked at me.

"I've considered it." The doctor's question startled me, but I knew he deserved an answer. At least it helped divert my eyes from Blaine.

Then a tap on a door before it opened. Alena entered, pushing a portable CT scan machine. She hugged me and then greeted Blaine. She prepared my leg for the scan while I laid back on the table. I questioned if I wanted to see the results. If it was a clot, I was in for another setback.

Alena pointed to the screen. "It's a clot, Doctor." Then she paused, "actually, it's two." She rubbed my arm, knowing my anxiety had just increased.

The doctor took a few minutes to view the screen, measure the clots, and revisit my file. Then he said, "you heard about the clots, so you know the ramifications if you don't follow instructions. I'm prescribing medication to help reduce the clots; hopefully, the body will absorb them. But if not, we'll go in again and get them."

I moaned because that was my fear. I've treated folks for clots and watched a few of them die when one took a path straight to the heart or lungs. Either way can be fatal.

"Here's the prescription and your instructions. Follow them to the letter. Then, be back here in seven days for a recheck." On the way out the door, he handed Blaine a copy of the instructions. "I'm sure you'll need a copy." Then he chuckled.

I sat on the table and winced as pain radiated to my hip. Alena tried to cheer me up, but I was still solemn. She hugged me on the way out and whispered in my ear that I shouldn't worry. The head of nursing should call any day, and Alena explained my recovery.

Nodding, I winked at Alena because she didn't know about the doctor's question about me. I didn't feel up to discussing it either.

Blaine helped me with crutches, and he left the hospital. As soon as he crossed the threshold, Blaine asked, "When were you going to tell me about the job?"

"I hadn't decided. I wanted to make sure I had the job before sharing." My head hung low because my leg hurt, my recovery was taking longer than I wanted, and I was still a target.

Carter and Hudson stood from the outside bench, confirming nothing unusual happened while we were away. I suggested a stop by the gym since I needed to visit a pharmacy before returning to the safe house.

We dropped my prescription off. Then we drove to the gym. Blaine hesitated to stop when he saw a black suburban parked at the door. He called Carter, and they discussed their options. He finally let Hudson visit the gym first. Since his arm still sported a sling, he'd use that as a ruse to look around.

Carter dropped Hudson at the door while Blaine parked a half-block away. Hudson returned within fifteen minutes of entering. When he climbed in the car, he said, "the black Suburban is the owner. He stopped in to grab the deposits. I met him, and he seems okay."

After Hudson described the owner, Blaine pulled into a space, and they exited. The guys followed me like bodyguards. Everyone in the place nodded at me.

I made it to the locker room, but Blaine entered first. Once he cleared it, he returned to the door and allowed us to enter. Our lockers were on the back wall in the far-left corner. As I lifted the lock, I hesitated. What would I find? Could I handle Casper's scent?

The guys noticed my pause and stepped back, giving me space. Blaine walked closer and stood next to me as his inner strength poured into my soul. I turned the lock to our three numbers, and it clicked open. My eyes riveted to the inside, resting on Casper's boxing gloves. Oh, how I remember seeing him spar. My gut clenched, and I thought I would fall to the ground.

Blaine stood behind me, holding me in place. "You've got this, Celeste. We're all here for you. Let's pack whatever you want to keep. Since you're moving, you won't be back here."

Carter and Hudson drew closer. "Did we hear that correctly?"

"Celeste applied for a job at the hospital. She had help from Alena." Blaine explained.

Carter's smile spread across his face. "That's the secret Alena has been keeping from me. Congratulations, Celeste. Let us know if you need help to move your things."

"I will, and thanks, guys. I'm unsure when I'll move, but it's in my future." I said, as I tried to keep the tears from flowing over the sides of my eyes.

Hudson had stepped away, but he returned with a plastic bag. "Here, Celeste. This might help with your things."

I nodded as I placed everything in the bag. Then the guys each took a turn searching the locker for Casper's list. It was nowhere to be found.

Blaine carried the bag to Carter's vehicle for me. "I'll search the bag for the list. Maybe he stuffed it into something."

They stopped at the pharmacy and then proceeded back to the safe house. While I endured another setback, it felt good to escape the house. The leaves blew gently against the wind as clouds passed overhead.

Carter eased the car into the garage first. Then Blaine followed. The door dropped before we exited the vehicles. I let out a breath that I didn't realize I had held. We strode into the house, locking us inside.

Blaine's phone sounded, but he didn't recognize the number. Finally, he answered, "Crosby."

Then we waited. "Ah, Commander Woodson, glad to hear from you. I take it everyone is okay from your ordeal."

The commander spoke for a few minutes as Blaine listened. Then Blaine said, "Commander, my unit is with me. Give me a second to place you on speakerphone."

"Everyone, take a seat. We have news." Blaine suggested.

I sat next to Blaine. Then the guys took the remaining seats. "We're ready."

"After we checked out at the emergency room, we returned to our original plan. We've collected soil samples, and we've extracted several plants. But I don't think you'll need Theo for the plants. They are hemp plants, and thousands of them are in this field. While scouting the area, we found another field, not quite as large as this one."

Blaine glanced at his group as they nodded their heads. "That explains why they wanted no one encroaching on their fields. Thanks for the update, Commander. Are you dropping the soil samples off with Theo?"

"He's waiting for us. But before we do that, we're stopping at Officers Davis and Porter's residence for a welfare check."

I grimaced because I could only imagine the payback they'd inflict on those two guys. Then Carter asked, "let us know what you find. We'd like a word too."

Commander Woodson chuckled as he ended the call. Then Blaine said, "finding that crop was the key to this whole mess. Now, if we could locate Casper's list, we could end the deaths."

"I'll search the bag, but I need to lie down." I picked up my crutches, but Blaine beat me to it. Instead, he lifted me and carried me to my bed. I rested my head on his shoulder, even for the short walk.

"Blaine, you're amazing. Thanks for the lift." He grinned as I dumped the bag's contents on the bed. Casper's scent radiated up to my nose, and I froze. I knew I'd never let go of those boxing gloves.

My fingers touched each article in that bag, coming away empty-handed. Where would he put that list? It must be at the house somewhere. Casper spent time in the garage with the punching bag and in his office. So, that list could be anywhere.

I heard Blaine answer his phone, but I couldn't understand him. Besides, I was too tired to get up and see what was happening. I figured Blaine would tell me if I needed to know. Next, I remember Blaine tapping on the door, telling me it was supper time.

"What? Supper. How can that be?" I muttered.

"You fell asleep, and we didn't want to wake you. Sleep is the best medicine. Commander Woodson called, and Porter and Davis were MIA. They've checked their residences and known hangouts.

Jancey placed a statewide BOLO for Porter as well."

"Amazing. Now both are in the wind." I fought my words because I wanted to lash out at the turn of events, but I didn't wish to Blaine take the hit.

I ate because I had to since my medicine required it. But, for me, supper was quiet. I had nothing to share, and I felt sorry for myself. My mind wandered into a dark place, and I couldn't figure out how to overcome it. The list remained a mystery. My leg caused more problems than I wanted, plus I couldn't decide on moving. Did I want to move away from my work family? Were they still my work family? I rarely heard from anyone, and the longer I stayed gone, the easier it would be to leave for good.

After supper, I ventured back to my room. I wasn't in the mood to socialize. The things from our locker were still strewn across the bed. I couldn't make myself pick them up, so I slept with them. When I awoke the following morning, I felt some relief in my leg. Maybe the medicine is reducing the size of the clots and releasing some of the pressure.

When I hopped into the kitchen, Blaine stood at the back window with his back to me. He had his phone to his ear. The guys sat at the table like they'd been awake for a while. My crutch smacked the corner of the kitchen island before anyone knew I was there.

All heads turned toward me. I muttered, "sorry."

Hudson jumped up to help me get coffee before I had to ask. He wasn't wearing his sling. "Where's your sling?"

"I removed it last night. I've started my exercises, and the doctor says I can use my arm as much as possible without causing damage."

Nodding, I wished I could use my leg. My hands and underarms were sore from using the crutches for so long, but since I felt relief this morning, maybe by next week, things will be better for me.

Blaine joined us in the kitchen. "We have good news. Theo called, and the soil samples taken by SWAT and our victim's shoes are a match. So I surmise our victim found the crop, but the killers found out and ended his life. It's like the killers are doing everything they can to protect this field."

"Wonder how much money it's worth?" I asked.

Everyone shrugged their shoulders. "No idea. But based on the number of plants, I'd say millions. And that's something worth protecting."

"Blaine, what about the small crop? Does it have the sandy soil too?" Carter asked.

"Yes, both fields have the added sand. Since our soil is dense, they add sand for water drainage."

All heads nodded. But we still have no idea who the head guy is, and that's where the list comes into play. Unfortunately, the more I consider the list, the less I know where to look.

While I enjoyed coffee and a bagel, the guys added Theo's information to their notes. Then Blaine's phone sounded.

He checked the caller ID. Then he tapped the speakerphone, addressing Jancey. "Morning. Another CI is in the hospital with a bullet lodged in his brain. He's in a coma. They found him on a downtown street near his apartment."

"I can't believe he's still alive. What are his chances?" I asked.

"Slim to none. There's been no movement and no response to pain stimuli. But the doctors say that could be his body's way of coping with the bullet. He's scheduled for an MRI today to see if the doctors can remove the bullet."

Carter offered, "it would be something if this guy recovered enough to ID his shooter."

Everyone agreed with Carter, then Blaine shared about the soil samples. When Blaine mentioned SWAT, Jancey chuckled. "Commander Woodson is still reeling at the fact one man rendered his entire team useless."

"That must have stung. But think about it, if the men were shoulder to shoulder in the truck and one was tased, the others would feel it. Electricity travels. Woodson said two of his men had burn marks from the tasers. Porter used the taser in its highest setting. He studied up on the tasers to know how to do what he did. I'm unsure if the rest of us knew the tasers were that strong." Blaine explained.

Jancey countered, "Porter didn't use our tasers. Instead, he used a more powerful one. Woodson found it in the truck."

"That's crazy talk. Porter planned this takedown well in advance or was ready whenever the need arose." Carter fumed.

They spoke for a bit longer, but added nothing else to the investigation. I wondered how many more CIs were on the list. "Shouldn't the police protect the remaining CIs? The department won't have enough left over after this is over." I stammered.

"Jancey is working on that now. Some SWAT members will help with the protection detail."

Then everything turned silent. The guys studied their computers, searching for anything to help us find this killer. I opted for a book and a quiet place to rest my leg.

I read until my eyes were hard to keep open. Then I started to rise when Blaine stopped me. He asked if he could help me with anything. I asked for

Casper's files. Maybe I could break the code if I can't find the list.

Blaine set me up with the file, pen, and paper and left me be to decipher my dead husband's words. My pen flew across a blank page, trying different combinations of letters. By the time I gave up, I had twenty pieces of wadded paper surrounding my seat. Finally, I yelled into the kitchen, "I need a computer!"

Blaine arrived first. "you need a computer. For what?"

"There must be a decoder on the internet. I can't figure it out manually, but Casper must have coded these on the internet. He didn't make this up." I explained.

Blaine left, then returned with his computer. We sat shoulder to shoulder, trying to decipher Casper's code. We found several that were promising, but they never satisfied us. Blaine was just as frustrated as I. If Casper had shared the list, I'm unsure if it would have meant anything to me. Finally, we ended our search, and Blaine returned to the kitchen to join the others.

Jancey called Blaine again. But this time, Woodson was on the line too. The guys discussed viable options to find the killer, but Woodson gave us the best idea. He said, "I've saved this for last because it's the most dangerous. The small crop is ready for harvest. I would think they would need to harvest it within the next seven days or risk losing the crop. If we can find spots for surveillance, we could arrest the folks that arrive to harvest. Maybe one will turn on the others."

Blaine's eyes met the others. Then Carter asked, "But the workers might not know who they work for, right? If that's so, we'll still be in the dark."

Jancey added, "It might be a risk worth taking. Unfortunately, we have no other leads to identify these folks unless the latest victim survives."

After a few moments of pondering the situation, everyone agreed to Woodson's idea. They'd work out how to surveil the field, but the worrisome issue is how to do it without compromising their location. Jancey advised the group they'd reconvene later in the day and discuss their options.

While I worked on the list and the code, the guys tossed ideas about the best way to surveil a crop in the mountains without being detected. They have ghillie suits which are used for these purposes, but everything was at the police station. That would leave me alone. Until I heard Hudson say he'd stay behind since he wasn't released from the doctor. I exhaled a breath because I wasn't ready to be alone.

Carter and Blaine prepared to leave, but before they did, Blaine sat with me. He whispered, trying to settle my nerves, but it didn't help. Before he stepped away, he pecked me on the cheek. That's when I decided I wanted more. I grabbed his arm as he stood and asked, "can I get a hug?"

He obliged and left me with a grin on my face. After that, I felt better but still worried about the surveillance.

Hudson paced as the guys left. He would stop repeatedly and jot down a note on his pad. I finally gave in and asked, "what's wrong, Hudson? You're concerned about something."

He stopped, facing me. "I am concerned. The killers could have explosives hidden near their crop fields, and no one would notice until it was too late. These killers are pros. We've seen their handiwork. I'm just trying to think of every scenario I can before the guys start surveillance. It appears surveillance will begin during daylight hours because we can't imagine anyone harvesting a crop at night."

"Unless they bring in their own light source," I added.

Hudson tilted his head, absorbing my comment. "For that to happen, they'd require generators and lights. But it's doable, Celeste. Now the question would be if anyone noticed the lights during the night?"

"I don't recall there being any cabins in the field's vicinity. It was nearly two miles from mine."

Hudson walked to the window and stared out of the backyard as he thought through the idea.

"There's a strong possibility these guys move the merchandise at night because they'd have less interference from hikers and less traffic on the roads. So I'm suggesting the guys surveil the field at night. But let's see what they say when they return." Then he added, "I'd like to be there to see how they harvest the fields. I bet it's truly amazing at these workers' speed, knowing they're messing with an illegal quantity."

Alena texted me to check on my leg. Then she asked about Carter. "Hmm," I muttered to myself, but Hudson heard it.

"What's up?"

"Alena texted me about my leg, but then she asked about Carter. Apparently, he hasn't called in a couple of days, and she's worried he's ditching her."

"Tell her from me that's not happening. He thinks he loves her but hasn't shared that with her, so don't spoil it." Hudson chuckled.

"I wouldn't dare. She kept my secret about the job opportunity, so I owe her one." I replied about my leg and Carter, hoping I satisfied her worries.

Hudson returned to the computer. His fingers flew across the keyboard now that both hands worked.

When I glanced at him, his chin rested in his hand as he read. I left him to it as I slipped off to do my exercises.

An hour later, I joined Hudson at the table. "Have you heard from the guys yet? It seems they should've called or texted by now."

Hudson lifted his phone, checking it to make he missed nothing. "Still nothing. But I'm sure they're busy if they're not already in place." He answered in a nondescript manner, but his insides told a different story. Blaine's lack of communication was troubling because that was so unlike him.

By mid-afternoon, Hudson felt he was waiting long enough, so he dialed Jancey. He failed to answer, so he left a message wondering what was happening. Hudson hated being left in the dark, even though he was still useless in the field.

At dusk, a car drove into the drive and sat there, causing a surge of adrenaline to run through Hudson's body. I noticed the change and questioned him. "We have a car sitting in the drive. I can't tell the make and model." Hudson took up a position at the front door because he couldn't cover every outside door in the house.

When he heard the garage door raise, he lowered his weapon and returned to the table. Blaine and Carter made it back. They entered with camouflage paint on their faces, wearing brown camouflage clothes to blend into their scenery.

I had never seen Blaine dressed, so it took my breath. He had a menacing look about him, as did Carter. But underneath the paint, they were exhausted.

Hudson spoke first, "thanks for the updates." He said it was using his sarcastic tone.

Blaine explained, "when we got to the woods, someone scrambled cell signals in that area. We tried to trace it, but we never found it. Jancey has already chewed us out, so if you don't mind, I'd rather not hear it from you."

Lifting his arms, Hudson stated, "sorry, man, we didn't know. But you had us concerned."

Blaine looked at me, "Celeste, do you recall if your cellphone worked when you were at the cabin?"

"Sure, it worked. I had to check in with Captain Swank weekly."

He nodded, then strode off to his room. We heard the showers running before Hudson acknowledged the cellphone scramblers. "What's the purpose of scrambling cellphone signals? Other than our guys can't call for backup."

"But the killers can't use their phones either, right?"

"I guess. So, are they preparing for the harvest? Do they scramble the cell signal before they begin?" Hudson asked.

As the guys discussed the case, I said little. Finally, after I had done my exercises, I crawled into bed and read. Sharp pain in my leg woke me, but as I rubbed it, it subsided.

Breakfast smells found my nose, causing my stomach to growl. I smiled because I knew who was at the stove and I wasn't disappointed. Blaine's back was to me as I entered, and I saw his muscles through his t-shirt as he flipped bacon and scrambled eggs.

When I sat at the table, he turned. "Morning. Can I get you coffee?"

"Absolutely, and good morning. I'm glad nothing happened yesterday."

"Me too. It will take more than just Carter and me to watch that crop. We're working on a plan to return tonight. I agreed with Hudson's comments about a nighttime harvest. Also, I need to thank you for that too. Hudson explained how you two worked through the scenario."

Blaine walked to me, bringing me a plate of food and steaming hot coffee. As he placed it on the table, he leaned down for a kiss. But this time, it wasn't on my cheek.

Between breakfast, coffee and Blaine, I was in heaven until my leg gave me another jolt of pain. I grimaced as I reached for it. Blaine watched but didn't move.

"What's going on with your leg? Do we need to see the doctor?"

"I had a pain overnight, but it subsided, so I'm hoping this one does too. The clots may be shifting. That could be good or bad." I explained as I rubbed my leg.

Blaine returned to the kitchen to grab his plate. Then we enjoyed a quiet breakfast alone. We discussed my job opportunities at the hospital and possibly moving. Blaine wanted to know for sure that I was moving, but I couldn't give it to him just yet. Besides, I have another interview before the hospital offers me a position.

"I have no doubt you'll get the position," Blaine said with a grin.

My positivity level wasn't as high as Blaine's, but I still had hope that I'd get the job. Then, I'd arrange to sell the house in Colorado Springs. But until that happens, I have no place to stay.

Before the others woke, I shared with Blaine my thoughts on moving. But, first, I needed to lay it on the table so he knew my status. When I shared, he said, "please don't worry about having a place to stay. You'll stay with me until we settle everything."

"I can't impose on you like that. I don't know how long it will take to settle everything."

"Time doesn't matter to me. You can live with me forever." Blaine shared as he held my hand.

His words shocked me as I tried to think of a reply. But Carter interrupted our discussion. Then, when he saw our faces, he asked, "should I come back later?"

Blaine winked at me, then faced Carter. "Nope. We're good."

I was grateful for Carter because I didn't have to respond to Blaine's comment. Then I remembered Alena. "Carter, Alena asked about you last night."

"I'll reach out today." So he said, but his tone sounded strange.

"Is their trouble in paradise?" I prodded as I stared at Blaine.

"Not on my end. I'm a little hesitant. I really like her, and I know I'll screw it up like I always do with women." He explained as he dumped creamer into his coffee.

"I wouldn't let that hold me back. She likes you, Carter. Keep the conversation going." I suggested.

Hudson joined a few minutes later. "Thanks for breakfast, Blaine. This is fantastic."

Carter looked dejected. "How come you think Blaine cooked?"

Hudson chuckled, "because he always does." Then everyone laughed.

The day progressed slowly as the men worked on the case. They had multiple calls, with Jancey as he worked on getting a team to the field tonight. Blaine and Carter would walk in around dusk, knowing things wouldn't happen until after midnight. The others would arrive around ten.

When the men left, Blaine hugged me and said he see me tomorrow. Somehow, that felt strange. A distant memory flitted into my mind as I'd heard the same comments from Casper.

As I laid my head down on my pillow, thoughts of Casper returned. Finally, I drifted off to sleep, thinking of our last snow ski trip and what fun we had together. Then, at three in the morning, I woke screaming for Hudson.

He raced into my room. "Celeste. What is it?"

"Look at my leg. It's on fire."

Hudson lifted the sheet and moaned. Then, finally, he touched it and said, "get your clothes on."

Then he turned and sprinted to his room. He was back in under three minutes. "I don't know what's happening, but someone needs to look at that. It's growing by the minute." Then, without asking, Hudson scooped me into his arms and carried me to the car.

Chapter 9

Hudson placed me in the back seat so I could raise my leg. After he slid my crutches into the floorboard, he climbed behind the wheel. He gave me one glance and reversed from the garage.

He flipped on the dash lights once we turned onto the main road. Then he expertly maneuvered the car between what little traffic existed, gliding the car through intersections with the red light glowing overhead. I'd have told him to slow down if my leg didn't hurt so badly.

Hudson drove the car to the emergency room entrance, the same place the ambulance had brought me last time, and bolted through the door. As his door closed, I moaned, then my head dropped to my chest because I couldn't hang on any longer.

When Hudson returned, he almost had a heart attack himself. Celeste passed out in his absence. "Hurry. She passed out." He shouted to the attendants, bringing the gurney.

They hustled to the car, and the men slid Celeste onto the gurney and wheeled her inside. After moving the car, Hudson raced into the emergency room to find Celeste, but the space was empty.

Hudson frantically searched for someone to answer his questions. Finally, he rounded a corner, almost knocking over a doctor. "Sorry. I brought Celeste Kerne in for issues with her leg."

"I know who you are. You have a bullet wound on your shoulder. I treated you when you came in. How's the shoulder?" The doctor inquired.

"It's fine. But I'm more concerned with Celeste. She woke me up about her leg." Hudson ran his fingers through his air, and the doctor understood the anguish.

"Let's go find out. Follow me." The doctor turned and strode off down the hall. They ended in a large room full of computers and people. Alena exited a door and made her way into the room when she spotted Hudson.

"Are you Detective Hudson?" Alena asked.

"I am. And you are?"

"Alena. I'm friends with Carter and Celeste. Why are you here? Is it Carter?" She asked with a tinge of concern.

"Carter is fine, I think. He's on a stakeout with Blaine. I brought Celeste in because of her leg. But I can't find her." Hudson sounded frustrated.

"Hold on. Doctor, did you find her in the intake log?"

"Not yet." Then the doctor looked at Alena, not understanding why her name wasn't listed.

"I bet they took her to surgery. Come with me, Hudson."

The duo trotted out the door and down another long hallway, an elevator ride, with another hallway. Hudson shook his head because he'd need a map if he worked here.

Alena stepped into the surgery office and found Celeste already under the knife. Then she explained the process to Hudson. The doctors were in the middle of performing a surgical thrombectomy where they would remove the clot surgically. Alena tried not to show worry, but she failed. Deep lines worked their way into her forehead.

"Hudson, tell me what happened."

He described Celeste screaming for him in the night. She held her leg when he walked into her room. It was apparent by the size of her leg that she needed medical attention. Hudson explained he drove her to the hospital.

"Well, thank goodness you were there. For a doctor to whisk someone with a blood clot into surgery, it's serious. But it looks like they caught it in time. Can you reach Blaine?" Alena asked.

"Not until they come out of the woods. All cell phone traffic is scrambled in the area." Hudson looked for a place to sit because he dreaded the idea of Celeste dying on the table. How would Blaine handle her death so soon after they met?

Hudson shook his head, trying to clear the awful thoughts. Then he walked off to the waiting room. Alena followed, but when they sat, she said, "I've got to get back downstairs. The surgery team knows of my interest in Celeste. They'll advise me when surgery is over, too. I'll find you." Alena patted Hudson on the knee, and then she slipped through the door.

During surgery, Hudson contemplated notifying Jancey about Celeste, but there wasn't anything he could do, so he waited. At least if he waited, he'd have news about the surgery outcome. So even though Blaine wouldn't receive a text, Hudson sent one anyway, alerting him to Celeste's hospital visit. The text would alert once the service returned.

What felt like hours was only fifty-two minutes, when a nurse explained that Celeste had a large clot in her leg, which Hudson felt was obvious, and the doctor removed it. However, they're concerned that a small piece of the clot that broke away, so Celeste will be in the ICU for twenty-four hours for observation and medication. The nurse promised to let me see her when she was in her room.

As the nurse left, Alena arrived, sporting a smile. "She did good, Hudson. You can relax."

"I won't relax until Blaine arrives. From what I heard, this is where the killers tried to get to you both." Hudson stated as he glanced at Alena.

Alena nodded as the memories returned. "You're right. But they have no idea she's here this time, right?"

"That's my hope." They sat in silence, wondering about the potential of the killer returning to the hospital. Hudson couldn't recall if anyone followed him to the hospital. He was more concerned about Celeste than about a tail. But if they did, they knew Celeste was back in the hospital. Hudson moaned.

At daybreak, Hudson's phone sounded. He smiled when he saw the caller ID flash Blaine's name. Hudson answered, then explained the situation. He also mentioned Alena sitting beside him. Then Carter said something about taking his girl away from him.

Hudson chuckled at Carter's comment, and he felt the tension leaving his body for the first time in hours. Now he felt exhaustion creeping into his body. Hudson told the guys to shower before they showed up at the hospital, since it was unnecessary to scare Celeste when she woke.

Shortly after the call, a nurse arrived, permitting Hudson to see Celeste. Alena led the way to the ICU, finding Celeste asleep. Every machine in the room beeped and gurgled as they worked to stabilize Celeste. Hudson sat in the chair beside the bed because he didn't want her waking up alone.

Once Alena checked in on her, she expressed gratitude to Hudson for saving Celeste's life. Then she left with the promise to return.

Hudson leaned back in the chair and fell asleep. He didn't know how stressed he was until he spoke with Blaine. He was unsure how long he slept, but stood from the chair when a noise jarred him awake.

It took him a second to remember where he was, but he recalled when Celeste croaked out a hello.

"Celeste. Thank goodness you're awake. Blaine should be here shortly."

I nodded, then I said, "thank you."

"Don't talk. You'll need that for Blaine. Just rest. Can I get you anything?" Hudson asked.

Then a commotion sounded in the hallway. Hudson tensed, and I was unsure what to do. Then we heard Blaine's voice, followed by Carter's. When Blaine entered the room, Hudson said, "you two sure are noisy." Then a pause, "where's Carter?"

"Alena was standing at the elevator. Carter picked her up and twirled her around. So they're catching up in the waiting room." Blaine smiled at the thought.

"Hudson, I owe you again. Maybe this time, the leg will heal."

"I'll leave you two alone. I'm going for coffee. Then I'll be back. You and Carter need to sleep. I'll sleep in the chair until you come back." Hudson explained.

I tried to talk, but the words wouldn't come because my throat was scratchy. Blaine placed an ice chip in my mouth, and I savored the coolness as it slid down my throat. Then I tried again. "I'm glad you're here. I promise I'm not this needy all the time."

"Celeste, I've told you before. I want you just the way you are. We'll get through this together." He squeezed my hand as I drifted off to sleep again.

The next time I awoke, Hudson sat in the chair with his head drooping, and Blaine was gone. I relished the fact my leg was pain-free. Something I haven't had since the injury. Maybe things were headed in the right direction for a change.

An unfamiliar male nurse entered my room as I lay in bed contemplating my life. He checked the machines but never touched them. Then I noticed he stared at Hudson, alerting my senses. While I didn't want to call Hudson's name, I needed him to wake quickly.

When I shifted in the bed, I grabbed the railing, making a creaking sound. The nurse backed away, and Hudson woke. He glanced at me, then at the nurse. Immediately, he felt the danger.

"Can I see your badge?" Hudson barked at the nurse. The nurse fumbled for it as he dropped something into his pocket.

When he passed the badge to Hudson, a tattoo on the underside of the man's arm at his wrist was visible. Hudson glanced at the tattoo, then back at the man. The nurse's attention turned to the doorway, as did Hudson's.

That was all the time the nurse needed. He ran to the door, but Hudson tackled him, and they fell through the doorway, sliding across the hallway. I picked up the call button for the nurse's station. When they answered, I asked for security.

Then a gunshot rang out in the hallway, and total chaos ensued. I couldn't see what was happening, but I heard the men, grunting and struggling. Then Hudson shouted at the nurse and another gunshot. This time, someone fell to the floor.

"Hudson?" No answer, and my heart sunk into my stomach.

Then I heard Hudson notify someone that the male nurse had a bullet wound to the torso. People rushed from the elevators into the ICU to render aid. The man spoke only in Spanish. I knew a little of the language, but he spoke so fast, I couldn't understand him.

Once they wheeled the nurse away for treatment, Hudson returned to my room. "oh, thank God. You scared me when you didn't answer." I said as I shifted in bed.

"It's a good thing you woke me. There was a full syringe in his pocket. My guess is he was here to deliver the contents to you." Hudson shook his head. "But what makes no sense is how they knew you were back in the hospital?"

I shrugged my shoulders, then said, "maybe they've been waiting for a return trip." Then a shudder ran down my spine.

Hudson sat in the chair after he closed the door. He dialed someone on his phone, and I heard Jancey's voice. Hudson rehashed the incident with Jancey, who was just as flustered as us.

After that call, Hudson took a deep breath, then called Blaine. Blaine's temper got the best of him as he described the series of events. He shouted, but he didn't aim it at Hudson. Blaine ended the call by telling Hudson he was on his way.

Hudson tapped the end button, then said, "well, just as I suspected. Blaine is mad and on his way."

"You handled it so he can stay at the house and sleep."

"That's not him. He'll be here within thirty minutes." Hudson spoke from experiences.

A nurse knocked on the door, and I froze. Would the killers enter with a gun first this time? Hudson had his hand on his weapon as he looked through the glass window. The nurse held her badge to the window and smiled.

Hudson opened the door as a greeting. She seemed to enjoy Hudson by making small talk with him while checking my vitals. The nurse spoke to me once, asking me if I needed anything. While she was in my room, she placed her attention solely on Hudson.

After she left, I said, "I think she liked you." Then I waited.

"What?" Hudson asked with a head tilt.

"You heard me," I said, chuckling. But, of course, Hudson had no clue that the nurse flirted with him.

Hudson moaned as he read a text. "The male nurse has no fingerprints. They've been burned off."

"That's crazy. Who would burn their fingerprints off?"

"Criminals. They make it harder for us to identify them. I'll run his photo through facial recognition when he gets out of surgery. If he's in the system, we'll get him."

Then Blaine entered the room. I noticed the dark circles under his eyes and the lines on his forehead. First, he gave Hudson a fist bump, then peeked at me on the cheek. "Are you okay?" he asked as he looked at me.

"Yes. I sure am going to owe you all a ton for saving my life so many times." I said as I held Blaine's hand.

Hudson spouted back, "you owe me nothing, but the others I can't answer for." Then he chuckled.

Blaine just smiled. Then he turned to Hudson, "do we know anything about our attacker?"

"We know he's a Spanish speaker with no fingerprints." Hudson raised an eyebrow as he described the male nurse.

"No fingerprints," Blaine repeated as he considered that statement.

Hudson continued, "our attacker is in surgery. I shot him in the chest after he tried to shoot me. We'll need a photo of him for facial recognition. That's our best chance of identifying him."

"Agree. Did you notify Jancey?"

"Yes, He was my first call."

Blaine tilted his head, "so, I was second." Then Blaine snickered. "Hudson, take a break. I'll be here a while."

Hudson nodded, then said, "I need to find a nurse." Then he laughed as he walked from the room.

"What does he need a nurse for?" Blaine asked. Then I laughed, sharing our earlier chance meeting.

Blaine nodded at my answer because he had a nurse too.

Blaine's text message alert sounded repeatedly. Finally, he fished his phone from his pocket and sat in the chair to reply. "It seems someone moved machinery to our stakeout field, so they must harvest at night. Both guys that watched the field after we left said they pulled lighting contraptions by four-wheelers."

"Sounds like they're preparing to harvest soon. Maybe tonight." I stated.

Blaine stared out the window, pondering the news. He would coordinate another surveillance night using the SWAT team. Based on the number of folks involved with the harvest, he'd need enough officers to surround the field. Someone was bound to try an escape, so he wanted to prevent that.

Hudson returned while Blaine spoke to Jancey. He walked over to Blaine and mouthed, "speaker."

Blaine stopped Jancey long enough to share that Hudson was here now. Then Blaine shared his idea of surrounding the field with SWAT. Otherwise, he feared people escaping custody. Jancey and Hudson agreed. Hudson wanted to be a part of it, but since the doctor hadn't released him for duty, he must remain on the sideline.

When the call ended, I interrupted. "Hudson, did you find her?" I lifted an eyebrow as I asked.

"Of course. Her name is Julie." Then he showed his phone. It was a contact card with Julie's name and number.

"Congratulations, Hudson." Blaine said as his phone rang. "Thanks. Hudson will be right down." Blaine looked at Hudson. "Our guy is out of surgery. He's waiting for his photo opportunity in the surgical recovery room."

Hudson grinned and waved as he trotted out the door. Then he poked his head in the room, "does anyone know where the surgery recovery room is located?"

We heard someone say, "I do."

Hudson turned and smiled, "never mind, I have an escort."

He left us alone, and Blaine faced me, apologizing for not solving this case quicker. I tried to butt in, but he refused to stop talking. He needed to get it off his chest. Then he admitted wanting to stay behind and guard me, but he knew he couldn't since Hudson was still on leave.

"Blaine, stop. No one questions how long it takes to solve a crime. But, you can't solve it without knowing those involved. We know that two officers helped the criminals along in this plight. And that hinders you from solving it. With those two guys out of the loop, things should settle for us because, with luck, there are no more officers on their payroll."

Nodding in agreement, Blaine looked at me. "Thanks, Celeste. Few people would accept what you've been through without bashing the police."

Minutes later, Hudson returned with several portrait photos of the attacker. Next, Hudson called someone at the office, asking for help on a facial recognition search. He forwarded the photos, and we sat back, waiting.

I pondered who the guy might be. Does he live here? Or did he travel from Mexico just to kill me? That's a wild thought. Why would someone spend the money to kill me? Is it the possibility of Casper's list? It would disappoint them to know that I don't have a clue about the list.

While the room was quiet, I dosed. I tried to listen to the guys' conversation, but they spoke so softly that it was impossible. Finally, I gave in to sleep. This time, I slept peacefully, without dreams.

When I awoke, the guys sat in the same place. "Any word on our guy?"

"Not a word. Sometimes it takes a while if the guy isn't from the states. But, since he seemed only to speak Spanish, we're assuming he's from Mexico." Blaine explained.

The guys grew quiet as my doctor entered the room, greeting everyone. Then he mentioned the altercation between Hudson and the attacker as he came to my bedside, asking me to move my leg and give him a number between 1-10 for my pain level.

It shocked me because I only felt a slight tug at the second incision. When I rattled off the number two, the doctor smiled. "Your pain level suggests that your clots have been forming since surgery. Now, recover quickly. Therefore, I'm releasing you, but you must wear these stockings for two weeks. No question. Then we'll see you again for another evaluation."

"Thanks, doc, for everything." I couldn't wait to get out of here, hopefully for good this time. When I swung my legs over the side of the bed, the doc placed his hand on my shoulder.

"Not so fast. You will still put no weight on that leg until I see you in two weeks. Then we'll discuss." His eyes penetrated mine to where I didn't talk back. Instead, I grabbed my clothes and crutches and hobbled to the bathroom to change.

Once I was out of earshot, the doctor gave Hudson and Blaine instructions, too. Again, I cringed because there would be no cheating in the system with those two around.

Two hours passed before a nurse rolled a wheelchair into my room. I gladly climbed in as

Blaine relieved me of my crutches. Hudson had gone downstairs earlier to scope out the parking lot. The guys figured someone was waiting to take the attacker's place, but we didn't know who that was yet.

Blaine asked the nurse to hang back at the door because I remained a potential target. She gave him a perplexed look as she pondered whether his statement was true. When I nodded, she stayed at the door. Once I climbed into the car, Blaine returned the wheelchair to her.

Hudson pulled in behind us, and we left for the house. "How does the leg feel?"

"It feels the best it has since the injury. I'm certain the clot began growing right after the first surgery. But, amazingly, it didn't explode." I shuddered, thinking about what could have happened.

"Maybe you're truly on the mend now." Blaine checked his rearview mirror every fifteen seconds, but I didn't question his actions. He has his reasons.

The house looked the same as when I left. Being back here felt good, and I headed for the coffee pot. "The hospital coffee is lacking in taste. Does anyone else care for a cup? If you do, I'll make a pot."

"Make a pot." The guys replied in unison.

Blaine took a call while I worked in the kitchen. I realized that my leg didn't hurt as it hung down. I smiled, knowing I had survived the injury. When Blaine ended the call, he smiled too.

"We have good news. The bullet we recovered from the hallway matches the bullets from the ground surrounding the cabin. So, that puts our attacker in the helicopter that sprayed us with bullets." Blaine explained.

Hudson nodded, then asked, "wonder how many people are on this guy's payroll?"

"Who knows? But it appears to be quite extensive."

The coffee gurgled as it filled the pot. I stood nearby, savoring the aroma while my mouth watered, waiting for a taste. "There was something I thought of while I lay in the hospital bed. I imagine Casper stored the list somewhere that would be close to him. He went to the office daily. Did anyone check his desk?"

"Captain Swank said the crime scene unit checked it, along with his partners. They found nothing but old files, and nothing pertained to the case."

"That makes no sense, Blaine. Wouldn't either of you keep a working file at your desk?"

Both guys stared at me and agreed. Then, Hudson added, "wonder if someone made it to his desk before the crime scene unit? Do they have cameras inside the police department?"

"I don't know, but that's a good question for Swank. They should have found it odd, too. So, why didn't they explore the reason?" This case flustered me in all aspects. My husband died because of it, I almost died, Hudson was shot, and we're still missing the coded list of players that Casper stashed somewhere.

I poured three mugs of coffee, holding mine with both hands. The cup's warmth felt good, helping to release some of my pent-up tension. Then, that first sip was delightful and well worth the wait.

Blaine asked, "let me help you to the sofa."

"Not yet. My leg doesn't hurt yet, and I'll need another cup." I grinned as we shared a glance.

He walked to the table and added the information about the bullets. This information placed the attacker at another scene, which helped with the case. Now, if we could identify him, it would lead to finding his boss.

Hudson returned from his room with his phone to his ear. He spoke about an appointment, so we waited to hear the results. "I have a follow-up appointment in two days. After that, if my range of motion is back, they'll release me back to work."

My eyes grew wide. "Don't worry. You'll never be alone. We can swap times now. Where is Carter?"

"He's visiting Alena. He'll return soon. When do you have a date with Julie?" Blaine prodded.

"Soon, I hope. She's checking her schedule for a night off. Otherwise, we might make it a breakfast date." Hudson snickered.

My mood shifted when I heard about Hudson returning to work. I didn't worry about keeping him from doing anything with his injury, but now I would. These guys had a life outside of guarding me and needed to enjoy it.

"I think it's time for you all to return to your life. I feel better now, and with a gun, I'll be fine on my own."

Blaine coughed, "not a chance. While we may move you to my house, you will stay nowhere alone until we solve this case. No questions." His voice was tense, so I knew not to further my comments.

Then we heard a car. The guys raced to the front door. Then they relaxed when the garage door opened. Shortly after, Carter entered with a smile on his face. He walked over to me, "so, how's the leg?"

I gave him the good news, and he complimented me on my recovery. "Do I smell coffee?" His head turned to the kitchen.

"There's a cup or two remaining. It's fresh too." I stated.

On his way to the coffee pot, he glanced at the guys. "Why do I feel like I walked into an unpleasant situation?"

I shrugged my shoulders as Blaine recounted my comments. Finally, Carter laughed, "Celeste, you should know by now we won't release you until the case ends. Besides, I don't see Blaine ever releasing you." Then he roared with laughter.

Hudson laughed too. Then Blaine faced me as he lifted his right shoulder. I laughed too, and it felt good.

Captain Swank called me to check on my recovery, and I explained about the blood clot. He couldn't believe I spent more time in the hospital, but he was glad things worked out. Then I asked about Casper's desk and what the crime scene unit had found. He confirmed they found old files. When I questioned him about that, he paused. Then he said, "I figured you would ask about that. Of course, no one admits to being in Casper's desk after his death, but I wouldn't expect them to if they're up to no good."

"Does your police department have cameras inside?"

"Only at the entrance and the jail side. There are none inside the detective's units." He stopped, then added, "but I wish I did."

"I agree, but like they always say, hindsight is 20/20." So we ended our call shortly afterward. Then I rehashed the conversation with the guys.

"No one admitted to being in Casper's desk. That speaks volumes. I wonder if more officers are on the take than Davis and Porter. Or if one of them took the files." Hudson offered.

No one spoke as they considered Hudson's comment. Then Blaine's phone blared its tone. He said, "it's the FBI." He tapped the answer button, stating his name and warning them the phone was on speaker for his unit.

The caller was FBI Agent Sarasota. She explained they identified our attacker as Esteban Hurtado from Mexico. He's wanted in the United States for multiple murders and brutal attacks in multiple states. My eyes grew wide when I heard his list of outstanding warrants. Then I shivered when I realized how close he came to killing Hudson and me.

Agent Sarasota continued as she confirmed a two-person team of FBI agents would escort Esteban from the hospital once he could travel. They are already at the hospital, and Esteban is sporting a new pair of silver bracelets as he's handcuffed to the bed.

Chapter 10

After the call with Sarasota, Blaine dialed Jancey. They spoke for a while, having a robust discussion about the case and surveillance. Blaine huffed and puffed as he went to his room. He stayed away long enough for Carter and Hudson to question the situation.

"Do you think Jancey canceled the surveillance?" Hudson wondered.

"How could he? We got nothing so far, and it's happening soon." Carter added.

I tried reading my book, but my mind kept wandering, so I gave up and stared out into the backyard. This ordeal has been going on for weeks. How much longer could this last? First, I have to get back home. Then I have a decision to make. But I've heard nothing from the lead nurse on a job offer. So until that comes in, everything for me remains status quo.

Blaine emerged from his room in fresh clothes. He walked to the table, then shared the latest. "Jancey gave us four more days for the harvest. Sarasota will stay here tomorrow night with Celeste. The three of us will go to the field. Hudson, you'll man our comms. Then, when you're released, you'll join the field team. Sarasota's FBI team plans on questioning Esteban when he wakes later. We must revisit what we have for the rest of today and maybe find the list."

We nodded in agreement, but I still had no idea where Casper stored the list. I prayed the harvest took place sooner rather than later. But the more I thought about it, the less I believed it would help the case, but I wasn't at a place to express my fear, especially since we had no other leads to find this guy.

The guys turned to their computers, and I looked at Casper's files again. There's a clue in the files, but I haven't found it yet. So I retook notes while reviewing the documents, hoping to uncover something new.

Halfway through the file, something gave me a niggle, but I couldn't pull it into my mind. What am I missing? I feel as if I should know the list location. Did Casper tell me, and now I can't remember? Why would that be so hard to recall?

The night ended, and we slipped off to our rooms. I completed my leg exercises and noticed they were getting more manageable, so I was grateful. It's incredible what continuous pain does to a body.

The following day, I awoke before the others. I started the coffee and hobbled to the back deck. When the sun peeked over the horizon, the colors were spectacular. Then I felt a presence. Without moving, a hand laid on my shoulder and gave me a gentle squeeze.

"Good morning. You gave me a scare when I couldn't find you." Blaine spoke softly.

"I couldn't resist the sunrise. Coffee should be ready." I said as I stood from my chair.

Blaine didn't move. Instead, he reached out and hugged me. I returned the hug with one arm, since the other held a crutch. As he released me, I muttered, "maybe one day I can give you a two-handed hug."

"I'll hold you to it." He kissed my cheek. Then he turned, heading to the coffee pot. The others were already standing in the kitchen, trying to figure out what to eat for breakfast.

Carter stood at the island and asked, "has the FBI interrogated Esteban yet? We heard nothing last night."

"I'm unaware if they did, but I'll follow up on it this morning," Blaine replied.

As the guys worked on the case, I became restless. Now that I felt better, I needed activity, but I didn't know what that was. So Blaine refused to let me walk the neighborhood streets, leaving me nothing but the back deck because I couldn't do the staircase down to the yard on crutches. So, I spent my day cleaning my room and the kitchen. It was nice to move around pain-free, but it wore me down. By mid-afternoon, the chore exhausted me, but the kitchen sparkled.

The guys planned their night, so they took naps during the afternoon. Agent Sarasota arrived after supper to stay with me. It was nice to see her, and we chatted some as the guys prepared their gear. She confirmed with the group that Esteban has yet to speak. A nurse delivered Esteban's clothes from his hospital arrival, and sitting on top of a plastic container was a cyanide pill.

Everyone's mouth hung open as Sarasota's comment resonated in our minds. This group was serious enough for the players to carry cyanide. That says much about the leader and how much they want to protect themselves from outsiders.

After the guys left the house, Sarasota suggested a movie. So, we settled in with our popcorn. Our night was uneventful, as were the guys. They saw nothing in or around the field all night, so it disheartened them when they arrived at the house the following morning.

Agent Sarasota left, and the guys climbed into bed to grab sleep while they could, since their plans included more surveillance tonight. That left me staring at the walls again. So, today, I tackled the family room by dusting every reachable nook and cranny. By week's end, I'd have the house shining.

Around noon, Blaine walked out on the back deck, greeting me. We discussed my night, then I asked about him. He's frustrated that the case has gone stagnant. Nothing new has happened in the past twenty-four hours; without a new lead, they're feeling the case of going cold.

"If it goes cold, where does that leave me? Looking over my shoulder for the rest of my life?" I asked with a tinge of concern.

"Not a chance. I'm not giving up on finding the killer." Blaine stated, leaving no question as to his intentions.

I just nodded because there was no reason to keep discussing the point. They'll solve the case, or they won't, and I'll have to live with whatever the outcome.

Just as Blaine stepped away, my phone rang. I didn't recognize the number, but I answered it anyway. I froze when the lady stated her name because I'd been waiting for this call. Blaine glanced back at me, and when he saw my expression, he joined me on the deck again. He was almost as nervous as I.

The lead nurse asked some pointed questions about my housing and my leg. When I explained about the clot and the subsequent surgery, she was comfortable offering me a position at the hospital, making more money than my current salary. I accepted her offer but stammered as I mentioned I was still on crutches. She chuckled and offered my start date to be in six weeks. Then I exhaled the breath I held.

Blaine hugged me as he congratulated me on the job, then he said, "are you ready to move your things from your home?"

I stared at him because I hadn't thought of that. I was still relishing the win of getting the job. "Give me a day or two to work through a plan. After that, I'd have to pack, contact movers, get with a Realtor, and do it all within six weeks."

"I'll help with whatever you need." Blaine leaned down, kissing my cheek. Then he strolled inside to eat while I considered my feelings about the job. I was happy about the opportunity, but I wondered if it was the right time.

Our nighttime schedule played out the same as last night. Agent Sarasota arrived at seven, and we waved to the guys as they left, with Hudson driving the crew as he returned to the field today. Then, we headed to the sofas and a movie.

Later in the evening, lightning flashed in the distance, but we heard nothing. Once the movie ended, we separated and headed for our rooms. In the early morning hours of the next day, I awoke to gunfire. It took a minute to figure out where it came from until Sarasota barged her way into my room.

"Grab your shoes and your phone." She looked at me, then added, "oh, and your crutches."

With my heart beating wildly, I followed the order. Sarasota stood at the door, peeking through the tiniest crack I'd ever seen. Then she whispered, "here's another one. Follow me."

She went into the bathroom and looked at the window. Without waking the world, there would be no way to bust that picture window. So, she returned to my bedroom. Sarasota glanced at me, then at the window leading to the side yard. "This way."

Sarasota forced the window up. Then she busted the screen out. "You go first. I'll help you get through it, then run as fast as possible to the neighbors. I'll be right behind you."

There was a sound at the bedroom door. Sarasota raced towards the door, knowing time was valuable. She pushed the empty dresser in front of the door, knowing it would only slow down the attack but not stop it.

I put my good leg through the window, reminding myself to land on it. Then, glancing over my shoulder, Agent Sarasota stood with her feet apart and her gun aimed at the door, protecting me as I worked to free myself from the onslaught.

The only thing I brought with me was my phone. There was no way I could carry a suitcase while I hobbled to the neighbors. I'd be lucky to make it to the neighbors with my speed.

I landed on my good leg, but it took all my weight, and I grimaced, praying it held me. A man shouted inside the house, and it brought more gunfire. Instinctively, I ducked my head even though they weren't shooting in my direction. Then, gathering my crutches, I walked as fast as possible, trying to separate myself from the attack. Before I made it to the next-door neighbors, I fell once, landing on my elbow as I protected my face from slamming into a rock.

I prayed my elbow held together because I needed it to walk. Unfortunately, the neighbor's house was dark when I made my way around to the front door. I had hoped they heard the racket and were already awake, but since they weren't, I pressed my fingers to the doorbell and waited. When they didn't respond after thirty seconds, I figured the house to be empty.

As I turned around, looking at my options, I grimaced. The house across the street had a car in the driveway, but I'd be out in the open as I crossed the road. Then I heard more gunfire, and it sounded closer. Maybe Sarasota cleared the house, and they're shooting at her. Should I go back and help her? Then I looked down. What can I do? I can't even save myself.

Sounds were getting closer, twigs snapped, and I knew I had to move. I headed for another house on the same side of the road, keeping to the trees. A shrill scream reverberated in the night air when I made it to the next house. I paused, waiting for the aftermath. When none came, I choked back a sob. Then I continued putting distance between the attackers and me, but I knew I didn't have long.

I remembered my phone, so I plucked it from my pants pocket. My finger sat poised over Jancey's number as I contemplated calling him. But with the night so quiet, I'd give away my hiding place, so I texted him instead. Then, the sound of footsteps.

I wanted to scream, but I knew I couldn't, and if I wanted to see this case closed, I'd need to fight to stay alive again. So, with my phone turned on vibrate, I kept waiting for it, but a reply never came. So, I sent another text to Blaine, but if I remember, they're in a dead zone.

A shiver crept up my spine when I realized I was alone. That thought jarred me to action, so I hobbled to the front door and almost cried. An eviction notice was taped to the front door, so I had no reason to believe someone was inside the house.

My shoulders screamed in misery at me as I pushed towards the next house. At least there were cars in the drive, so I assumed someone would be home. Now, I had to wake them. I pushed the doorbell but heard nothing. Since I couldn't tell if it worked, I turned to the cars. I prayed they were locked, and the alarms set. But when I smashed a window, I had to hide because the attackers would know my location.

I plucked a rock from the flowerbed and reconsidered my idea. Glancing around the neighborhood, I didn't see another option. Then it hit me. I needed to set off the house alarm. But I didn't know how to do that without busting a window. A car window would be easier to replace than a house window. What would I do if the car had no alarm?

Then I heard it. Whispering. The guys were in earshot of me. I dropped behind the bushes, hoping they'd continue their search. But where is Sarasota? Panic overtook me as I struggled to catch my breath, knowing I'd never win this battle.

As I lay on the cold, damp ground, my body ached as my muscles were sore from the exertion of getting here. I wanted to find Sarasota. Would they think I'd double back? Without thinking through the idea, that's what I did. Once I no longer heard the whispering, I stood and hobbled across the house's front, hoping they continued in the back.

When I turned the last corner, I moaned as I found Sarasota with two gunshot wounds to her chest. She bled out where she lay. I leaned over and closed her eyes. Then, knowing there was nothing I could do for her, I followed my path to the house on the far side.

If I could separate myself from them enough to make a call, I'd call 911. But unfortunately, neither Blaine nor Jancey has responded to my text messages. As I crossed between the houses, I saw a man looking in the windows of the house I had just left. I shivered.

I froze where I was because any movement would draw unwanted attention, and I had no place to hide. So when they moved further away, I worked my way to the house with the car in the drive. I know a family lives here because I've witnessed them come and go for days.

Keeping my body close to the house, I reached the front door. Then I pressed my fingers on the doorbell and waited. When the first light appeared, I left the porch because my presence would cause the attackers to turn on these unsuspecting homeowners.

A man answered the door, but finding no one, he returned inside, turning out the lights as he made his way back upstairs. After I gave him time to settle back in bed, I repeated my process. First, I aim to have him call the police to check around his house. But I didn't know how long this would take.

After my second round, the activity brought the attention of the attackers. When I heard them talking, I hobbled to the backyard, returning to the darkness. The attackers stood on the drive when the homeowner opened the door. He yelled at them to get away from his cars. Then he slammed the door. If I could just hold on for a little longer, the police would arrive.

I made my way to an outdoor shed and huddled up behind it. I shivered as the cool night air seeped into my bones. The sweat I generated added to my discomfort, but I couldn't chance being seen. I hoped the homeowner would scare the attackers, and they left.

A few minutes later, I heard no sirens. Did the guy refuse to call the police? How is that possible? I plucked my phone from my pocket, seeing the time. It had only been an hour, but it felt like ten. I texted Jancey again, followed by Hudson, Carter, and another one to Blaine. Someone has to see these because I can't do this all night.

The nighttime silence continued as critters started making their noises again. That gave me peace that the attackers had given up on finding me. But did I chance coming out of my hiding place? With several more hours until daybreak, I stayed put.

I couldn't tell what time it was when I heard screeching tires and car doors slamming. Sometime in the night, I must have fallen asleep, dozing with my head against the shed. Then I felt my phone vibrate against my leg.

Tears poured down my face as I read Jancey's text. I worked my way out of the neighbor's backyard, finding Jancey standing in the house's drive, looking around for me. He ran to my side when he spotted me hobbling toward him.

"Celeste. Thank God you're okay. Where's Agent Sarasota?"

Before I could answer, more tears poured, then the sobbing. Instead of speaking, I pointed, and we walked to her body. Jancey's temper exploded. Finally, he calmed enough to call the FBI office to explain the situation.

"Celeste. How many men were there?"

"Two. One looked like Esteban, so much so that it was scary. I didn't know what else to do. The neighbors slept through gunfire, and I knew if I called someone, they'd hear me. I'm so sorry Agent Sarasota is dead." Then I crumpled to the ground. How many more folks will die because of this case?

Jancey looked around. "Blaine and the guys are on their way too. Let's get you inside."

Before that happened, two cars flew down the road and skidded to a stop at the driveway. The guys raced from their vehicles, still wearing face paint and work wear. "Celeste," Blaine called my name as he ran my way.

He took me by the shoulders, then asked, "are you okay? Do you need to go to the ER?"

"I'm not going back there, but I would like a shower." He chuckled when he saw my clothes.

"We all need to do that." Jancey stared at us as he worked to decipher our relationship. No one offered to explain. Instead, we walked to the house.

I headed to the shower while Jancey explained my night. The guys paced the kitchen when they found out about Sarasota's death. A heavy vehicle sounded, alerting them to a new arrival. They met the medical examiner's van at the drive. Jancey discussed the situation with them and Agent Sarasota's body location. When the team heard about the agent, their heads drooped.

First responders are one extensive family, and they never like to hear of another's demise, much less transport the body to the morgue. That's a rough trip, even for the most tenured person.

I returned from the shower, finding everyone gone. A small part of me panicked at the thought, but the front door opened shortly after. The men entered with solemn expressions, and their shoulders slumped. I knew the reason.

Something in me made me apologize to the group for Sarasota's death. My eyes filled with tears, but I kept them at bay as the guys told me it wasn't my fault. Of course, they can say that all day long, but could I accept it?

I made coffee while the guys showered, and Jancey worked on his phone. After three calls, I lost count. My mind returned to Sarasota as I saw her body in a blood pool on the ground. Would the memory ever subside?

Once the guys returned to the kitchen, they joined Jancey and me at the table with their coffee. Jancey wanted to meet with them before they slept. He asked Blaine to describe their night.

"Apparently, while Celeste was fighting her attackers, we were arresting field workers. We captured them all, but there were no leaders, only workers. They have their harvesting down to a science. If we hadn't interrupted their plans, they could have harvested the entire field in three hours, which says a lot because that field was dense with the product."

Then Carter added, "the workers are in holding cells until we can interrogate them. But, unfortunately, they speak Spanish."

Jancey made notes on the overnight raid, but disappointment clouded his eyes. "So, what do we have? I see nothing except a dead FBI agent. Come on, guys. You're the best in the business." He stood as he raked his fingers down his face. "I need something. Anything."

Hudson raised his hand. "I have an idea. It's not on the field, but Celeste. If these guys drove their car and walked the road, doorbell cameras would have that information for us."

Jancey's head bobbed. "I like it, Hudson. Make it happen today. I know you're sleepy, but this is of utmost importance."

Hudson agreed to handle it this morning. Then the others offered their assistance, too. With everyone involved, it would happen quicker. I sat back and listened, as I couldn't shake the feeling someone was watching me.

After Jancey left, Blaine walked over to the sofa and sat beside me. "I'm sorry you had to go through another escape in the woods. I should have stayed here."

"No, because it might be you laying on that slab in the morgue. I can't believe Sarasota is dead, Blaine. I just knew she'd join me in the woods." My voice cracked, but I held back the tears.

"What do you remember about the attackers?"

"One guy looked like Esteban, but I knew it couldn't have been him. Please don't think I'm crazy when I say this, but I feel like someone is watching us."

Blaine's head snapped around. "Guys, we might have a bigger problem. Instead of telling the men my thoughts, Blaine jotted in on a notepad. He's concerned that if someone planted a camera in the house, a microphone isn't too far away.

That means someone listened to everything Jancey said, and if they can't find the camera and mic, they need to move.

The team stepped on the back deck to discuss business while I searched for the camera and mic. Blaine called Jancey and explained my thoughts. Jancey promised a crime scene would stop by and sweep for bugs. When they returned, I was still searching. In my search, I found nothing, and then I patted myself on the back for my cleaning habits, as I'd already taken care of the cobwebs.

Hudson worked on the computer to find the nearby homeowner's contact information. He worked from the deck in case there was a bug. Carter helped make calls, too, while Blaine assisted me in the search.

Blaine found a camera sitting on top of a candle on the mantel. It was the tiniest camera I'd ever seen. It was amazing, it worked. Then we continued looking for bugs. Since I'd never seen one up close, I was uncertain what they looked like, but I kept plugging along.

When I reached the coffee table, I glanced down as I maneuvered my crutches around it. I spotted a round silver thing that resembled a battery stuck to the underside of the glass tabletop. "I think I have it," I whispered.

Blaine walked over for a glimpse, then the guys followed. They agreed the object I found was a bug. I was proud of myself. Blaine removed it, deposited it in a plastic bag and placing it in the garage. He'd let the crime scene tech inspect it.

By the time Blaine and I found the camera and bug, Hudson had contacted three of the eleven homeowners. Two have doorbell cameras, and the house on the right corner as you enter the neighborhood has a full-blown surveillance system. Carter offered his find, too. "I have three with cameras and one more call to make."

So far, out of eight contacts made, we have one surveillance system and five cameras. All heads nodded, because the outcome pleased them. Three homeowners were unavailable, so they left messages.

Blaine pulled out a chair and plopped down. "Now, if they would just send over the video, we could watch it, then take a nap. I'm beat."

Carter and Hudson nodded too. I was sleepy too, but it scared me that I'd see Sarasota's body every time I closed my eyes. So, sleep would come later for me.

A few minutes passed before email alerts sounded. Hudson clicked his email open and smiled. "here's the first one."

He clicked the link open, starting the video. We watched as a black SUV passed the house. The tinted vehicle windows prevented us from seeing the occupants. But I knew my attackers were in that car.

We watched the same video multiple times to make sure we overlooked nothing. We didn't because there was nothing to see. I hobbled off to the kitchen for coffee. Then I propped up against the counter while the guys discussed the case.

Then, the guy's fists bumped into each other. Finally, Blaine exclaimed, "Celeste, we have a tag number."

"Really?" I said, grabbing my crutches for a trip to the table.

Hudson played the video again, pointing out the vehicle in question, then the tag number as they parked on the street, two houses up from our home. While the tag sat at an angle, the license plate was visible.

"How soon will we have the owner?" I asked, clearly eager for the outcome.

"Carter entered the search already. We're waiting." Hudson explained.

Then Carter spoke, "the car is registered to a rental car company. We'll track the renter from there." Carter entered the rental car company's name into his search bar, producing a contact number. He dialed and explained his situation to the person on the other end of the call.

We waited while he went through three people before finding someone that could help him. Finally, he stated his request again, and they offered a name. It shocked Carter when they said Enrico Hurtado. Then he clarified the name, but the sweetest gesture was when the car rental person offered to email Carter a copy of Enrico's US driver's license.

I wanted to reach through that phone and hug that person. This is exactly what we need. We smiled as we waited for the email. It took longer than expected, but it was worth the wait.

Carter clicked the attached picture, and we gasped. Enrico could pass for Esteban's twin, but the birthdate on the driver's license, if it's real, puts Enrico two years younger than his brother. The driver's license is from California.

"Do you think they live in California, or is this license fake?" I asked.

"Most definitely, the license is fake. Then I wonder why he would use his real name and photo?" Blaine pondered.

Chapter 11

I typed Enrico's address into my maps app. Then I moved to the satellite map. "It looks like a nice apartment complex."

"What does?" Blaine asked.

"Enrico's address. Here, look for yourself." I turned my computer around to face them. They came closer for a better view. Blaine zoomed in on the complex.

"Maybe I was wrong on the address, and he lives here. Let's ask Jancey for help on checking it out." Blaine returned to the table for his phone. He dialed Jancey and explained their latest tidbit. Jancey agreed to call California, asking them to conduct a welfare check.

Hudson was speaking on the phone when Blaine ended his call. We waited for Hudson to finish. Instead, he jotted notes before he told us the outcome. "A homeowner with a doorbell camera called. She's sending the video to me. I have one homeowner that I haven't heard from. What about you, Carter?"

"I'm waiting for a return call, too."

Blaine nodded, as they probably have the best videos of the attacker already, so he wasn't concerned with the two remaining calls. However, his ringing phone broke his thoughts in half as he answered.

His head bobbed as he listened to the caller; it was good news by his expression. "Esteban is awake. We're free to ask questions."

Hudson spoke, "I'll stay. You two go on over there before they change their minds."

Blaine replied, "thanks, Hudson." Then he pecked me on the cheek as he followed Carter to the door.

"They'll need a translator. We can speak a little Spanish, but this guy has a different dialect because I understood nothing he said. Office Miller speaks Spanish. Maybe he could help them out." Hudson sent Blaine a text with the suggestion.

Hudson napped while I read. The time moved slowly with the guys away. I didn't want to wake Hudson, so I moved to my room. Then I noticed that this was the only room I hadn't cleaned. So I removed Casper's items from my bed one at a time. When I got to the boxing gloves, I placed the gloves under my nose and inhaled deeply.

As I breathed in his scent, I could see him pounding on the boxing bag at the gym. He always wore a scowl on his face when he boxed. I guess it's the intimidation aspect.

I wrapped the ties around the glove, noticing something white sticking out from the wrist area. After I tugged at it, it refused to budge, and I didn't want to destroy it. Instead, I took it to the bathroom so I could get my tweezers. With the tweezers in hand, I worked to free the white thread, if it was a thread.

While working on it, I noticed that someone had made a small slit in the glove inside the wrist. My heart rate ticked up a notch as I knew this was what we had searched for. Once I pried open the sides, the tweezers slid inside just enough to grasp the note.

Then, when it finally came out. I exhaled because I couldn't open the note fast enough. I stared at the list written in Casper's handwriting. We had it, but I didn't want to wake Hudson, and I couldn't share it with Blaine and Carter. Well, there's nothing like waiting when you have something good to share.

I read each name on the list. Then I refreshed my memory on the file. This was major and could blow this case wide open. I knew I'd have to turn this over to Blaine, but I wanted a copy in case something happened to it.

After locating my backpack, I pulled paper from the inside and scribbled the list on it. Then, I hid it in my backpack in a waterproof compartment because I wasn't taking any chances of losing it.

Returning to my cleaning, I completed it with gusto. My energy level was soaring with the list finally in our hands. Finally, the guys can finish this case, and I can get on with my life. But unfortunately, I had only four weeks until I started my new job, and I had a lot to do.

With the end in sight, I searched for realtors in my area and noted names and numbers. I made a checklist of what I needed to accomplish before I started my new job, and finding a realtor was on the top. Propping up on pillows, I leaned back on the headboard and started dialing.

I wanted to discuss my situation with several realtors before deciding on the one I'd use. Unfortunately, only one took my call out of four tries. After explaining my case, the Realtor instructed me on the best way to handle things. She seemed knowledgeable and caring, so I promised I'd wait until she sent me a market analysis of my home.

When the call ended, relief was my first thought. I'd begun working on my next chapter in life. My ordeal proved that life's changes are inevitable; once you accept them, you will come out on the other side.

Hudson stuck his head through my door. "Blaine and Carter should be here in ten."

"Good. I've got the news." I beamed as I wrestled with my crutches. "They're stuck."

Hudson chuckled, "it looks like they slid under the bed. Hold on. I'll get them for you."

He leaned over and pulled the crutches out from under the bed. Then he held them for me to grab. We wandered into the kitchen to make coffee when the garage door opened.

The side door opened just as the coffee pot gave its first gurgle. The men looked exhausted. Hudson couldn't wait, so he asked, "what happened? Did you get anything out of him?"

"It's a good thing you suggested, Officer Miller. Without him, we would've been lost. Miller translated Esteban's words, but he gave us nothing to help. Instead, he's worried about living and repeatedly asks for his cyanide pill."

"That's so sad," I said, then continuing, I plucked the note from my pocket. "I have news."

"What's that?" Blaine inquired.

"This is the list we've all been searching for. I found it in Casper's boxing glove by accident." I unfolded it and handed it to Blaine.

He smiled and offered his congratulations. "This is fantastic. It appears Esteban and Enrico work for their uncle, named Rodrigo or Rodi. But I'm uncertain if he's the leader or just a step in the hierarchy."

"Rodrigo is a name I recognize from somewhere else. Let me find the file." Carter stated as he rushed to the table. He flipped papers until he found what he needed. "Here it is. Rodrigo is mentioned several times in a file about an undercover drug sting. So, if Rodrigo is the leader, then he's responsible for Casper's death."

All eyes turned to me, and I blinked rapidly, trying to stop my tears from overflowing. I finally had a name. "Where is Rodrigo?" I stammered.

"No one seems to know where he lives. That's part of the reason for the drug sting. They were trying to draw him out in public so they could arrest him. But it seems he has others do his dirty work for him." Carter explained.

Hudson pointed out, "since we have names, we should speak with Esteban again. Threaten his uncle and brother."

Blaine nodded as he pondered the information. "I'm unsure if that would matter. If they carry cyanide pills, their devotion to their leader is serious."

Carter offered, "let's try it, anyway. At least he would know that we know about his background. It might give us a little leverage."

Jancey called Blaine, and he put the call on speaker. Blaine explained the note with the list of players. Jancey couldn't believe the news. It thrilled him. Then he said the field workers were ready for questions. They were set up in the conference room at the office. He suggested the guys visit Esteban and then come to the station for the workers. As a bonus, he told the group to bring me to the station while the three guys spoke with the field workers.

I glanced at Blaine. "Now, what am I to do in a police station while you all speak with this group?"

Blaine chuckled, "we'll get you another book. Also, take your computer. We might need help."

I returned to my room, grabbing my backpack. Then I chastised myself for not making more copies of the list. I put that on my follow-up list.

We drove in two cars because we were unsure what to expect. Since we found the cameras, I've felt like someone watched my every move. I scoured my bedroom several times for cameras or mics, but I found none. So maybe I was being paranoid.

I stayed in the car with Hudson while Blaine and Carter revisited Esteban. When they returned, they told us about their visit. Without Miller, they asked a nurse to translate. Esteban still refused to give them anything useful. But his eyes flickered when they mentioned the name Rodrigo.

Blaine was in a foul mood. He felt like he wasted time revisiting Esteban, but that's part of it. Next, they headed to the police station so they could interview the field workers. While he expected nothing from this group, they still had to interview them.

Jancey met the group at the doorway. "Celeste, you'll be in here." He pointed to the office next to his. I glanced at Blaine, and he gave a slight nod. I slipped inside, closing the door.

Then I heard Jancey ask Blaine about the visit with Esteban. "There's not much to say. Esteban refused to divulge any information, but he flickered when we mentioned Rodrigo. He knows him, but he never admitted it."

Jancey brushed it off and suggested they begin with the workers. He brought in other officers to help with the interviews. Blaine grimaced because he wasn't fond of bringing in outsiders. These officers weren't privy to the information Blaine's unit had developed. But he understood Jancey was trying to help.

Blaine turned to Carter and Hudson, "we need a questionnaire, so all parties ask the workers the same questions. Let's put one together. Then we can start."

The guys strode into the conference room, finding nine officers sitting around the table. "Thanks for helping. We're putting together a questionnaire because we have certain topics we'd like answers to, so give us a few minutes, and we'll get started." The officers nodded in acknowledgment.

Hudson typed as Blaine and Carter rattled off questions. Then Hudson asked, "shouldn't we ask about their boss? No one mentioned that."

The guy chuckled, "I would add that question since it's important." Carter stated, then looked at Blaine. "how did we overlook that one?"

Blaine shrugged, "because we're rushed for time."

Once they finished the questionnaire, they made enough copies for every field worker. Blaine stood at the conference room table and instructed his group. "Each field worker will have one questionnaire. There's room for notes too. Let Carter, Hudson, or I know if you run across one willing to talk. Also, if you have questions, let us know. Thanks."

The group split, taking a stack of forms with them. Next, Jancey placed fifteen workers around the station in different offices, allowing us to meet them individually. Then we rotated for new workers. While the process was slow, it was necessary.

I stepped out of my office periodically for a break. Blaine spotted me on one trip to the ladies' room. "Hey, is everything okay?"

"Yeah. It's fine. I just need to move around a little."

"Last I looked, we should be on the downward side of the interviews." Then multiple officers raced for the elevators.

Blaine asked, "what's going on?"

"There's a massive pile-up on the interstate, and the state police requested assistance." An officer said as he stepped into the elevator.

I looked at Blaine. "sounds like you might be here a little longer than you thought."

Blaine didn't reply; instead, he huffed and puffed as he strode toward Jancey's office. I carried on down the hall. Pictures of fallen officers hung on the wall, and memories of Casper returned. Would his picture be on the wall in Colorado Springs?

Blaine, Hudson, and Carter completed the interviews that the others didn't. Finally, Carter called the others to a corner for a chat. "I may have something here, but the man is so nervous, I can't get him to tell me what's wrong."

"Maybe he needs a softer touch." Blaine trotted off.

I entered the room with Blaine, and the guys smiled as they understood his comment. "Maybe Celeste will get it out of him. Introduce her to the worker. Then, let's see what happens."

Carter ushered me into the room, and in the corner sat a frightened man. I entered on crutches, and the man stared at me. I offered my hand when Carter introduced me. He shook it, but I felt the trembles as his nerves coursed through his body.

I spoke softly and slowly. His name is Antonio. He's been working in these fields for three years. Antonio was plucked from his Mexican factory to come to America. They promised him great riches for his family, which he hadn't seen. I asked about his family, and he froze. Now, I knew the reason for his nervousness.

"What happened to your family, Antonio?" I asked.

He looked me in the eye and muttered, "I don't know."

"Are they still in Mexico?"

He shrugged, "my wife and son might be, but my daughter is here in America."

I assumed she was a worker too, but tears poured down this man's face when I asked. Since I found no tissues when I scanned the room, I asked Blaine to get us a box. I left the man alone while Blaine was away. When Blaine returned, he handed the tissue box to Antonio.

Once the tears subsided, I asked, "why the sadness when you mention your daughter?"

He shook his head vigorously from side to side. I glanced at Blaine. Then he added, "Antonio, we can protect you and your daughter. Then we'll work to get your wife and son to America, if that's what you want." His eyes grew wide as he listened to Blaine's offer.

I suggested giving Antonio a minute to decide. We stepped out of the room as Hudson walked toward us. "I have a man that says we need to speak with Antonio, that he might help us."

"That's who we have in there. He knows something about his daughter but hasn't told us yet. So we're still working on him." Blaine explained.

Carter's eyebrows bunched. "how old is Antonio's daughter?" Then all eyes focused on Carter.

"Oh, no, Carter. Do you think these monsters took his daughter for themselves?" I asked.

"That's exactly what I'm thinking. Why else would Antonio not share information about his daughter? He's fearful for his life and hers."

Blaine raked his hand down his face. This is the one case that has been troublesome from the start. "Celeste, go back to our guy. See if you can prod any information out of him. We'll stay out here."

I returned to the room, and this time, Antonio paced. He was taller than I thought, but skinny. His face was dried with tears, and his eyes were clear.

Antonio made his decision. "Celeste, I'm ready to talk. I can't do this alone."

Smiling, I patted him on the arm. "Let me get the guys." I hobbled to the doorway, opened the door, and called for the guys.

They joined us immediately. I asked Antonio to start at the beginning. We needed his hometown in Mexico, his family members' names, and how he made it to the states. We jotted notes as fast as we could to decipher the pertinent information.

An hour later, we had it. Antonio worked in a factory in Mexico when some men entered, plucking folks from their worktables. His daughter, Maria, worked beside him. She's only fifteen. When Antonio yelled she was his daughter, that made it worse, he hadn't seen her since that day, but if he didn't do exactly what the boss said, they threw Maria's name out there because they knew he'd do whatever to keep her alive.

Blaine's hands balled into fists as Antonio described these men and what they make the workers do. The boss flies these workers to different fields when the harvest is ready. They're never in the same place long. The boss has fields all over the west coast. The largest is in Colorado, so most of their time is in the state.

Then Carter mentioned the murders. Antonio nodded. "he knew nothing about those. But Varga might. He works with me, and he told me one night he heard one of the men say something about a murder and how someone witnessed it."

No one looked at me, but I knew my expression had given it away. Then, finally, Antonio's eyes met mine. "It's you. You're the witness."

I nodded because I couldn't find the words. Then I asked, "would Varga speak with us?"

Antonio shrugged his shoulders. "I'm unsure. You'll have to ask him, but don't mention my name."

Blaine asked us to meet outside. "Antonio, we'll be right back. Can I bring you anything?"

"Coffee. I have had none since I left Mexico. All we drink is water."

I grimaced at the thought of not having coffee. These men were the truest form of the word monster. Once we cleared the door, "we must save Maria. I can't imagine living like that for years."

"We will, plus his family in Mexico. I wanted to step out and update Jancey. He needs to help with Antonio's family." Blaine said before heading to Jancey's office.

Then he stopped and directed his attention at Carter. "Why don't you grab Hudson and interview Varga? You know what we're after." Carter nodded as Blaine shut Jancey's door.

While the men were busy, I wanted Antonio to enjoy a fresh pot of coffee, so I made one. I stood by as the pot gurgled because I wanted no one to touch it. This pot was Antonio's. He could drink the entire pot for all I cared.

When it finished, I asked Jancey's assistant to help me carry it to Antonio. She was an older lady who had been with Jancey since he started. He was like a kid to her.

Antonio's facial expression showed nothing but yearning. Since I was unsure how he liked his coffee, I brought creamer, sweeteners, and flavors. He was like a kid in a candy store, uncertain which to try first.

I sat in the corner and let him explore his options without saying a word. Antonio deserved this for what he's been through. He closed his eyes as he savored that first sip. Then he released a sigh.

Holding his cup with both hands, Antonio said, "I'm sorry for what you saw. No one should see something like that."

"You're right, Antonio. It was scary, and it turned my life upside down. I've been in hiding since." I shared. "Blaine and his unit are good at what they do. They've saved my life twice. They'll do what they say too, and not everyone is like that. Give them a chance to find Maria and protect your family. Do you want them to travel to America, or are you returning to Mexico?"

Antonio pondered the question as he sipped another cup of coffee. "Wherever is the safest place? Those people know where my family lives in Mexico, so I know I can't return there."

Just as he finished, the door opened. Blaine and Jancey entered. Jancey shook Antonio's hand, then asked, "do you have a picture of Maria?"

"No. When they took me from work, they took all our things. I've had no wallet, money, or phone since that day." He lowered his head as the memories rushed back.

"Ok. We'll find her without it. How can we find your wife and son?" Jancey asked.

Antonio raised his head and looked at Jancey. "really?"

"Yes, we're going to Mexico to get them and bring them to you."

Antonio jumped up, grabbed Jancey's hand, and began shaking it. Jancey glanced at Blaine because the shaking wouldn't stop. When Jancey pulled his hand free, Antonio apologized.

"No apology needed." Jancey handed him a pad of paper and a pen. "Can you give us their location?"

Antonio accepted the pen but studied it before writing the requested information on the pad. It obviously had been a while since the man had touched a pen. As he handed it to Jancey, he said, "my wife has photos of Maria."

Blaine spoke, "perfect. We'll ask for one from your wife."

Jancey stated, "give us a little time, and we'll be back."

The men slipped out of the room, leaving me with Antonio. After his second cup, he asked, "can I have one more cup?"

"The pot is yours. Then I can make more. Just don't make yourself sick of it. There is always coffee in the states." I let the silence linger as Antonio tried a flavored coffee this time. He smiled.

A few minutes passed before Carter and Hudson entered the room. They admitted to having a productive interview with Varga, but opted to wait for Jancey and Blaine before sharing. Then they stepped out for a break, asking for a text when Jancey and Blaine were free.

As I sat in the chair, my thoughts returned to the day I witnessed the murder in the field. I saw no one else other than the two men with the victim. Then I wondered who said something in front of Varga. I found it odd that the killers would talk in front of a worker unless they suspected the worker would never get to tell his story.

Blaine returned to the room alone, "Carter and Hudson finished their interview with Varga, but they wanted you and Jancey to hear the information." I advised.

"Ok." He closed the door on his way out. While I wanted to hear the outcome, the guys needed the opportunity to discuss it without Antonio hearing it. My phone beeped, so I plucked it from my pocket and smiled when I saw Swank's name.

He texted me for an update, and I paused because I didn't know where to begin. So much has happened. So, I gave him a synopsis, which turned out to be a lengthy text. My phone rang seconds after sending the text.

Swank called because the case updates shocked him. He couldn't believe everything that had happened. So we spoke for a bit longer, but I ended the call when the guys entered the room.

Blaine spoke first. "Antonio, we've arranged for transportation of your wife and son to the states. We're placing you in protective custody until this is over, and you'll stay in one of our safe houses until this case is over. Jancey arranged for your family to join our WitSec program, too. But we need one more piece of information."

Everyone inhaled, waiting to hear the last piece of the puzzle.

Antonio tilted his head as his eyes shifted from Blaine to Jancey. "We need the name of the boss or no less than the shooter's names."

"The shooters are Edgar Guerrero and Martin Rosales. But two brothers, Enrico and Esteban Hurtado, were also involved in the murders. At least that's what Varga said. I'm not sure about the boss' name, but the brothers act as if they own the place." Antonio's nerves caused his leg to bounce.

Jancey paused, then said, "we'll make the arrangements, Antonio. Please let us know if you think of anything else to help us."

Blaine motioned for me to follow him. I did after I told Antonio I'd be back. "His story checks out with Varga's, so we're keeping him, too. The other workers will stay locked up until we finish the case. We can't afford for them to die because of our raid."

"Can you find the boss with the shooter's name?" I asked, because that didn't seem like a lot of help.

Blaine lifted his shoulders. Then he added, "I hope so. ATF, FBI, and US Marshalls are working on this case now. The other departments became interested in it when we asked questions about a drug cartel operating in Colorado. Supposedly, the ATF was already under suspicion of one, but they hadn't shared with anyone else until we came along."

"Maybe someone will recognize the name in one of your groups." I nodded, thinking that might work.

Jancey called us from his office door. I followed Blaine and the guys because I wanted to hear the update. "ATF volunteered to send a plane for Antonio's family. We've opted not to call them in case someone tapped their phones. Instead, they requested we have Antonio prepare a recorded video for them, advising them to go with the ATF officers." I nodded because that's something I can handle.

He handed Blaine a note with a number scrawled on it. "That's the number to text the video, too. They're leaving here at 7:00 pm. That gives you two hours to get the video to him."

"It won't take that long, sir." I turned and hobbled off to Antonio's room.

When I entered, it startled Antonio. It seems he's constantly on edge, but hopefully, that will subside in a few days. I explained what we needed, and he was more than happy to comply. We scripted his message, and then we practiced. On the third try, we succeeded. I had the video within thirty minutes of leaving Jancey.

I texted it to Blaine so he could send it to the ATF. Then we were in a waiting game. Antonio ate supper, but it wasn't easy to swallow. So I finally asked what they ate.

"Mush."

I almost choked on his reply. Then, without a response, I let it go. These poor people, how can anyone mistreat another person so badly? Will the drug cartel let these workers return to their lives, or do they kill them when they're no longer needed? A shiver ran up my spine.

Blaine received a text advising the plane had landed safely in Mexico. They waited for confirmation that the ATF had Antonio's family safely on board a flight to America. The scheduled rendezvous to the chopper was estimated at two hours.

As the day lasted longer than normal, my body told me to rest. But I pushed through it because I wasn't missing this reunion. We sat around the conference table eating supper, watching Antonio enjoy his first American meal. He asked for pizza. Jancey splurged by ordering multiple variations for Antonio to try.

Antonio ate off and on for two hours. He seemed oblivious to the time. But Blaine wasn't. He kept touching his phone, waiting for the time to show. I could tell the delay was causing anxiety in all the men. No one brought up the issue, but it was there.

Blaine stepped from the room at the three-hour mark, with Jancey following. My insides rolled as my pizza settled in my stomach. Somehow, I knew something had happened in Mexico, and I struggled to look Antonio in the eyes because I didn't want to be the one to share the news.

When Blaine returned, he carried a slight smile. Antonio faced him. "is everything okay?"

"Yes. There was a gunfight in the streets around your house, but the ATF unit has your wife and son and is on their way to the plane." Blaine's eyes never wavered, but I saw something there. Was it uncertainty?

While we waited for word on the escape, Blaine and the guys finished with the other workers. No additional interview provided usable information other than Varga. Since he wasn't married or had children, his situation was manageable.

I propped my leg in another chair and leaned my head against the wall. Then a thought struck. Varga verified the shooters as Edgar Guerrero and Martin Rosales. He followed with the names Enrico and Esteban Hurtado. Yet, somehow, they connect to this drug cartel too.

I opened my photos app and found the picture I made of Casper's list. I found all the names Varga mentioned. Then my eyes flew to the name Felipe Hurtado. So that's the leader we're looking for, and Rodrigo works for him, too.

I texted Blaine that I had information. He showed up within seconds of my text. Blaine slid a chair beside mine so I wouldn't have to move. Then I explained my news. First, I pointed to the picture of Casper's list, then said, "it makes sense if Felipe is the leader. Remember when Antonio said that the brothers acted like they owned the place? Well, they're part of Felipe's family. So, in essence, they own a part of it."

"You're brilliant." He said as he leaned over, pecking me on the cheek, then racing out the door.

I grinned as he left, knowing I had helped in a small way. But when I checked the time, my smile fell away. The ATF unit had plenty of time to make it to the airstrip. They chose this one because it was the closest to Antonio's house.

Chapter 12

Without waiting for Blaine to return, I texted him the question about the ATF unit and the plane. He replied, "we've heard nothing." My stomach took another flip.

I laid my head back and closed my eyes, not expecting to sleep, just rest. But my body had other plans. I fell into a dream-filled sleep, with gunfire bouncing off the conference room walls. The bullets came closer every time, and I ducked as they whizzed by my head. Finally, someone shook me, and when I opened my eyes, Antonio stared at me with a confused look.

"Sorry, Antonio. I fell asleep and had a nightmare." As I straightened up in the chair, the men entered. They were tense.

Blaine explained. "there was another delay at the airport, but they are on their way to America. Depending on the weather in southern California, they should arrive in two hours." Antonio beamed with pleasure as his eyes filled with tears.

Hudson and Carter left as Blaine sat beside me and exhaled deeply. "What happened at the airport?"

He whispered, "When the unit arrived at the plane, their pilot lay dead in the cockpit." Blaine took his hand and raked it across his neck from side to side. "Luckily, one of their unit members flew helicopters while he was in the service. It took a few tries, but he finally felt comfortable flying it. The best part is everyone is safe, except the pilot."

"Wow. It's amazing any of them made it out of there in one piece. Now, I can't wait for the reunion. Have you found anything on Felipe?"

"Yes. That's what Carter and Hudson are doing now. They're meeting with the drug unit and more ATF and FBI agents. It seems this man moves around often because he fears for his safety."

I nodded because I would, too, if I were in his place. There's probably a bounty on his head at all times. Now that I know his identity, I'm unsure if I want to meet him because if I do, I'd like to kill him. And I can't do that.

Blaine's message alert sounded. He grinned when he read it. "Antonio, they've landed at the airport. It's about an hour's drive from here."

"Thank you, Detective Crosby. Without you, I would have never gotten the chance to see my family again." He hugged Blaine while patting him on the back. Then he reached for the last piece of pizza.

I studied the man and wondered where he put all that pizza. Then I chuckled because seeing someone this happy makes me happy.

Blaine escorted Antonio to the men's room, allowing him the chance to freshen up before seeing his wife. Antonio fidgeted as he paced the conference room. Then concern crossed his face, and I suspected it scared him his son wouldn't recognize him. He told me his son was almost eight years younger than his daughter.

We heard a commotion outside the room. Antonio looked at me, and I met his eyes. I gave him a slight nod of encouragement.

Blaine opened the door, motioning for me to leave. I passed a petite lady with shiny black hair and tear stains as I left. I turned my head to the boy. His eyes were enormous as saucers as he took in his surroundings, and he looked just like his father. There would be no problem with recognition.

When the pair entered the room, we listened to the threesome reconnect. There were tears and shouts of happiness. Thirty minutes passed before Antonio tapped Blaine on the shoulder, "here's a picture of Maria." Instead of taking the picture, Blaine snapped a picture.

"Thanks, Antonio. Does your wife or son need anything?"

"Not right now. But we are tired." He gave a slight grin.

"I bet. We are too. Let me check on tonight's arrangements." Antonio returned to his family as Blaine spoke to Jancey.

The thought of helping someone reunite with his family after all this time was undoubtedly the best thing I have ever witnessed. I hoped Casper saw it, too.

Two ATF agents volunteered to stay with Antonio for the night. Then we'd reconvene in the morning. Once they left for their safe house, Blaine led me out of the station and into his car. "I want to take you to my place, but I can't, since this case took an unexpected turn."

"I want to finish it too. Felipe Hurtado needs to pay for all the deaths he's caused."

Blaine held my hand as he said, "he will."

We drove to the safe house, with Carter and Hudson following. Carter's light flashed twice, alerting us to danger. Blaine pulled into a grocery store parking lot, and Carter pulled alongside. "Hank from the ATF just texted me. They have a black SUV following them at a distance."

"Tell them we're on our way and to use no radio traffic. If he needs anything before we get there, he needs to call your cell phone. Ask Hudson to call mine, so we have an open line?"

"Celeste, get in the back seat and lie flat. That's the safest place to be." Without questioning him, I exited the front seat, climbing in the back and lying flat.

Then the tires spun as they grabbed asphalt, following Carter onto the main road. The guys didn't use their lights and sirens for fear of alerting the black SUV. Two miles later, they spotted the SUV. Carter raced up the truck's side so Hudson could view the driver.

"It's a woman."

"What did you say?" Blaine barked.

"A woman is driving the SUV."

From the backseat, I yelled, "it doesn't matter. She could be a part of the drug cartel."

Then Blaine repeated my sentiment, changing their tactics. He confirmed with the others to treat the woman as hostile. So, that's what they did.

When the time was right, Carter raced past the SUV, sliding to a stop in front of the truck. The truck's brakes locked as the heavy vehicle skidded to a stop within a foot of Carter's vehicle. Hudson and Carter took positions on the opposite side of the car with their guns aimed at the occupants.

Carter yelled for the driver to exit her vehicle with her hands above her head. He concentrated solely on the driver but heard people talking behind him.

So, he said to Hudson, "get these people back. They're in the line of fire."

When Hudson turned around to yell at them, Officer Miller pulled behind their vehicle, separating the onlookers and leaving Hudson with Carter. Carter noticed Blaine at the back of the SUV, waiting.

The driver finally slid from the SUV, keeping her hands in the air. The passenger followed by exiting the vehicle with his hands in the air. Carter took the driver while Blaine handcuffed the passenger.

Carter grabbed the women's left wrist and brought it down behind her back. When he snapped the cuff, she turned, wielding a knife. Hudson yelled. The driver slashed the knife toward his face, but he deflected it. Instead of his face, she struck his forearm.

When Carter bent over holding his arm, Hudson shot the driver mid-chest. She crumpled at Carter's feet. Blood poured from Carter's gash as he worked to stem the flow.

Blaine walked his handcuffed suspect around the vehicle, and the turn of events shocked him. He wasn't prepared to see Carter cut and the driver with a gunshot. Blaine left his detainee with Hudson and trotted back to the car.

"Celeste. The driver slashed Carter's arm. Can you help until the ambulance arrives?"

Blaine grabbed the medical kit from the trunk, carrying it for me. We found Carter holding his arm above his head, but the blood ran down his arm into his shirt. "Let me look, Carter."

He lowered his arm for me. Then I cleaned his arm with what little antiseptic I had, and I applied a pressure bandage. By the time I finished, we had heard sirens coming our way. "You'll need stitches and a tetanus shot if you haven't had one recently."

"Thanks, Celeste. I appreciate it." The ambulance pulled in behind Office Miller's vehicle. Hudson had our passenger crammed in the backseat of Miller's car. So he could watch as his partner gets a ride to the hospital.

The EMS guy walked over, rolling a stretcher in front of them. "What do we have?"

Blaine explained, "the victim has one gunshot to the chest. She's semi-conscious, and her pulse is steady."

"Ok. We've got it from here." The EMS guy kneeled as they worked to stabilize her. They loaded the driver within three minutes of their arrival. "It looks like she'll make it."

"We'll be at the hospital shortly," Blaine explained. "Can Carter ride with you? She sliced his arm, and he needs stitches."

"Sure. Come on, Carter. Grab a seat up front."

Carter nodded at Blaine and Celeste, but as he walked past Hudson, he gave him a fist bump. We knew that was for protecting Carter. Hudson potentially saved his life.

Hudson drove Carter's car to the station as he followed Officer Miller. We followed them after a tow truck arrived for the black SUV. Hudson escorted the passenger to an interview room. I hobbled off to the washroom so I could rid my hands of Carter's blood.

Blaine met me at the door. "Hudson and I are interviewing the driver. I'll find you when we're done." He squeezed my hand as he turned and strode away.

With sweat on his brow, I glanced through the two-way window and noticed how nervous this guy was. Maybe this is the weak link.

Hudson handed me a file before we entered. "Another guy with the name Hurtado? How many are there in this world?" Hudson chuckled but didn't answer.

I returned to the office next to Jancey's while the guys spent time with the truck's passenger. Then I remembered the two-way window. I could watch the interview and maybe help.

While the guys perused the guy's background, I watched him. They had his hands bolted to a bar connected to the table, but his feet were free. The guy was large in stature, with small black eyes that matched his hair. They lifted a weapon from his waistband with a filed-off serial number. There's always a reason for that, and it's never good.

As Blaine read the file, he'd glance at the guy, and more sweat appeared. That gave Blaine something to work with. Time was on his side.

Hudson and Blaine began the interview. The guy refused to speak. He wouldn't even shake his head. They continued like this for hours. The only flicker of recognition I saw was the mention of Maria. He knew where she was, but he wouldn't tell.

Hours and hours flew by as the men continued berating this guy with questions. Finally, Blaine and Hudson had the luxury of leaving the room for a break, but the prisoner didn't. Instead, he sat in that straight-back chair the entire time.

The guys stepped out of the room for a bite of supper. They'd been at it for eight hours. Over pizza, they discussed their tactics and the new ones they'd employ when they returned.

I returned to my post as Blaine and Hudson returned to the room carrying water bottles. The guy's eyes showed yearning. He was starving and thirsty. Maybe this will help him talk. Blaine took a swig from his bottle, then Hudson did the same. The guy watched, hoping that the third bottle was his.

Blaine offered, "this is yours, provided you share what you know about Felipe Hurtado and Maria."

"He'll kill me."

"Well, your option is to starve, thirst to death, or start talking," Hudson said through clenched teeth.

Carter entered my room with his arm bandaged and dark circles under his eyes. "You need to sleep. With your blood loss, you're bound to be tired."

"I am tired, but I'll rest when this is over. We're too close to slow down now. Besides, I've heard the caution before as Alena stitched my arm."

"Uh oh. How did that go?" I asked, cringing.

"About like you'd expect. She wasn't happy about it, but as she said, it could have been on the operating table." Carter said with a slight grin.

I nodded because that's true, too. Then, we watched the suspect ask for the water bottle.

Hudson said, "we're waiting."

The guy shifted in his seat. Then he started talking. Hours into the interview and he finally starts sharing. "It's about time," I muttered.

"Maria travels with Felipe, along with several other girls. They're arriving in Colorado in the next twenty-four hours because of the havoc happening here. Felipe wants to visit his nephews."

Blaine shook his head, "that will not happen. We'll get to him first. Now, tell us where he'll stay."

The guy paused but exhaled a breath, giving up Felipe's address. He described the house's layout but said he's only been there a handful of times over the past ten years. When I heard that, I stammered, "ten years."

Then Carter asked, "how many girls could he have mistreated in ten years?" He shook his head as he tried to come up with a number.

Blaine stuck his head in my room once he had Felipe's information. "Oh, hey, Carter. How's the arm?"

"I'll live. I want in on the raid." He stated.

"Ok. I'm headed to meet with Jancey. Then we'll break for a few hours. If Felipe isn't due in for twenty-four hours, we have time to put together a solid team and grab some sleep." Blaine added.

Carter nodded as Blaine winked at me. He left, followed by Carter and Hudson. I continued watching the suspect. He fidgeted more than ever, but I couldn't determine the reason. Finally, he stood from the chair, leaned over the table, and put his mouth to his hand.

I screamed for Blaine as I rushed into the interview room. The suspect swallowed a cyanide pill, and I needed to get it out of his mouth quickly. The guy's eyes were wide when the door was pushed open because he knew he was out of time.

Using one hand, I squeezed both cheeks, causing his lips to pucker. The pill sat on his tongue, or what was left of it. Blaine raced into the room with the others in tow. "What's wrong?"

"He tried to swallow a cyanide pill. I watched him work to get it in his mouth before I realized what he was after. So I stopped him from placing the pill under his tongue. However, the pill sits on his tongue, and I can't get my fingers in there to retrieve it." So I paused a second, then barked, "Guys, make him open his mouth."

Hudson walked up behind him and punched him between the shoulder blades. The punch forced the man's mouth to open, allowing me to grab the pill. "I got it." Then I added. "the pill should have been under his tongue, but we acted quickly. He might feel sleepy, but the cyanide should dilute with an IV of fluids."

"He needs a trip to the ER, then?" Blaine asked.

"Definitely."

Blaine called for an ambulance, then updated Jancey on the incident. When he arrived to inspect the scene, he said, "Celeste, thank you for saving that man."

I nodded because that's what I do. I'm a nurse, and once you're a nurse, you're always a nurse.

Once the ambulance carted the guy away, I needed coffee. Blaine graciously brought me a cup before he returned to Jancey's office to finish their discussion on the case. Blaine dropped into a chair across the desk from me when they finished.

"Can we leave now? You're exhausted."

"Yes, let's leave before something else happens." He put my bag over his shoulder, and we headed to the elevator. Carter spoke to someone on the phone as he walked up behind him. He smiled when he saw us.

We climbed into the elevator, leaving Carter leaning against the wall. The silence in the elevator was golden. Neither spoke on the ride down.

Blaine looked both ways before letting me out the door. "Don't you think with the collapse of Felipe's army that I'm in the clear?" I asked because I start my new job in a few weeks and need time to handle things in Colorado Springs.

"We're close. But I'm not letting you out of my sight until Felipe dies or is in a cell." Blaine stated in a terse tone that he's known for. When he uses that tone, there are no follow-up questions.

Overnight, I slept so hard that I felt a million times better the next day. But Blaine beat us to the kitchen. When I reached the kitchen, I said, "I thought I would beat you to the kitchen this morning."

"Not a chance. I slept so hard last night that I woke up early. So here's your coffee, and pancakes are almost ready." Blaine said with a smile. Then we turned when he heard footsteps.

Carter showed, then Hudson. I gasped when I saw Carter's arm. "Carter, your arm. It's bleeding again."

"I know. I hit it in the shower last night. It's not bleeding now. I don't think." He said, looking at it.

"Walk over to me. Let me look. We need fresh bandages anyway." I glanced at Hudson, and he headed for the bathroom where Carter kept his stash.

By the time he returned, I had Carter's bandage off. The wound was a mess. He had bled more than he thought. But once I cleaned it, I could tell there were no broken stitches. So, he should be fine, but I'll need to monitor it for bleeding.

Once everyone had eaten and showered, we returned to the station. The group met with ATF, US Marshalls, and the FBI on a takedown plan for Felipe. They figure they'll need the people to surround the house, and, by the looks of it, the house isn't small.

Since I was locked away in my room again, I contacted my boss at my previous hospital, letting them know about my new job. While they didn't want me to leave, they never expected me to return. I wish someone had told me that because the decision to leave would have been easier.

Glancing at my leg, I couldn't wait to put my foot on the floor. I had another few days before I saw the doctor again. If he gave me the okay to walk, I'd head to Colorado Springs to pack what I needed. Then I'd have the Realtor meet me to sign the papers to get the house on the market.

Blaine mentioned me staying with him, but I think it's too soon, so I'd need an apartment. That thought sent shivers up my spine. Why? Did I not want to live alone? Or would I push Blaine away?

Thoughts raced through my mind as I doodled on paper instead of tackling my list of things that needed to happen so I could move. After several minutes of second-guessing myself, I shook off the feelings, knowing I had a place to go.

Several hours later, Blaine opened the door, "we have a plan. Are you ready to hear it?"

"Of course I am. The sooner you all capture this guy, the sooner we can get on with our lives." Then I lifted an eyebrow.

He took the seat across from me, then described their plan. "We'll have a team of fifty agents from

ATF, the FBI, and our department. It will be an overnight attack, probably around 3:00 AM. We agreed the goal was to capture Felipe alive, if possible. But it's a must that we rescue Maria alive."

When I heard that, it made my heart happy. "That's what I needed to hear. Maria is the most crucial."

Then Blaine acted like he had something to say, but it troubled him. So, I asked, "what's wrong?"

"You'll need to stay the night here since we set the op for overnight, and I have no one to stay with you at the house. I'm sorry about that. The third shift officers will know you're here if you need anything."

"I can drive to Colorado Springs and stay with Captain Swank if you think it's best." I offered, even though I didn't want to.

"I'd rather you stay here because I don't think I could stand knowing you're traveling alone for that distance." Then he waited for my reply.

Nodding, "I'll stay. But I want all doors locked. You know we have outstanding BOLOs on two of your officers." His eyes grew wide at my statement.

He lifted his hands and bolted from the room. Then I chuckled because they forgot about their officers. What would the odds be if they returned tonight and found me locked away? I wasn't in the mood to find out.

I made a few more calls, then Jancey stood at the door. Then Blaine's head poked in over Jancey's shoulder. Jancey said, "pack your things. You're staying with me tonight."

Words wouldn't come, so I stammered, "I am?"

"I've already told my wife. She'll have supper waiting for us." I stared at Jancey and gave a slight nod. But I felt uncomfortable staying with him.

He left Blaine standing at the door, then I asked, "no other options, huh?"

"Not this time. We'll be back early enough that you can be here when we arrive. Jancey agrees to bring you to the station with him."

My agreement was a simple nod. "Thank you for your understanding. I know this ordeal has been terrifying for you, but know it's almost over." He leaned over and kissed my cheek.

Blaine stood at the door when Jancey pulled out of the lot with me in the passenger seat. It was a strange feeling, but at least I wouldn't be alone and could sleep in a soft bed. Jancey said little as he listened to the radio chatter. There was a fire from an auto accident and a missing kid.

"I don't know how you do it, Jancey." The words flew from my mouth before I could stop them.

"It's in the blood."

I nodded, as I could understand that feeling. It was just like nursing.

He turned into a middle-income neighborhood with manicured lawns and streetlights. His house sat at the far end of the main neighborhood road. The front porch light glowed as he parked the car.

When we reached the front door, he opened it with a keypad. I nodded, understanding his safety concern. His wife stood at the counter when he entered the kitchen. My stomach immediately growled at the aroma. Everyone looked at me and chuckled.

"Hi, I'm Martha. You must be Celeste. We'll eat in a few minutes, but first, let me show you to your room. You can drop your things in there and freshen up." She never questioned my crutches. Instead, Martha took me by my elbow and chatted about the house as she ushered me upstairs to an enormous bedroom. This room had its bath and sitting area. I almost wanted to ask if I could rent it.

The evening was pleasant, but my mind wandered back to Blaine. I feared for his safety and those of his coworkers. Then the image of Maria filled my mind, and I cringed. How would her parents handle the news if she wasn't found with Felipe?

When the time came for bed, I was ready for some alone time. Martha was like my grandmother, thinking food and drink solved the world's problems, but then she spoke of the hard times she faced being married to a cop. After she said it, she looked at me and apologized.

"There's nothing to apologize for, Martha. Death is a part of life. It's inevitable. My husband's life was taken too soon, that's all." I patted her on the hand as I stood. She helped me with my crutches. Then I hobbled off up the stairs.

I was grateful when I reached the landing. It allowed me to catch my breath before I tackled the rest of the stairs. My phone rang the next to the last step, and I hurried to answer it because I wanted to hear from Blaine before I went to sleep. As if sleeping was even a possibility.

Chapter 13

I answered the phone a little out of breath, and Blaine asked, "are you okay?"

"Stairs. I'm in an upstairs bedroom." After I settled my breathing, "How are you?"

"I'm ready to have this operation under my belt. All total, we have fifty folks prepared to swarm Felipe's house. It's amazing how many people want to see this guy behind bars. But I really called to tell you good night, and I'd see you in the morning."

"Thanks, Blaine. I needed to hear your voice." Things were moving so fast for us that I seemed to get closer every time I stepped back.

Once the call ended, I lay in bed, staring at the ceiling. I couldn't turn my mind off. The incident which started this ordeal for me circled back to Casper. I wouldn't be involved if I'd never gone to the mountains. Casper would still be dead, and I wouldn't have met Blaine. It's as if Casper put me with Blaine because he wanted me to have someone.

That was my last thought until 3:00 am, when I woke with a start. I had no idea what woke me up, so I checked my phone for messages or missed calls. I had neither. Maybe my mind reacted to the time because of the raid. I glanced at my clock again, only 3:05, and wondered if Blaine was okay.

I dozed off and on for a few hours, finally giving up at 6:00. Jancey was taking me to the police station, and I didn't want to be late. So I showered, dressed, and packed before heading downstairs. Instead of hopping down the stairs, I slid down the stairs on my rear. It was quicker and far easier for me.

When I entered the kitchen, Mr. and Mrs. Jancey sat at the table with their coffee. "Good morning. Have you heard anything?"

"Nothing yet, but it's early. We'll leave here shortly. Try to eat something and have coffee."

I nodded because the lump in my throat prevented me from speaking. Martha handed me a full mug of coffee. I smiled, then stammered with, "thanks."

After eating a muffin and drinking half my coffee, I felt better. But I wanted to hear from Blaine. So Jancey turned on the police scanner, and we listened to it crackle. There were two traffic accidents in town, one with injuries.

Once breakfast ended, Jancey was ready to head out. He opened the door for me. I turned and hugged Martha for her hospitality. Then we walked to the car. Halfway there, Jancey stopped, staring up the street. I stayed still as he worked through his thoughts.

"Hurry, Celeste." He barked. So I followed instructions. I moved as fast as I could on crutches.

Sitting in the passenger seat, I glanced at Jancey. Finally, I couldn't take the suspense, "what's wrong?"

"While walking to the car, I saw a flash of light, like a rifle scope. But I see no unusual vehicles, so we're taking the long way to the office. Buckle up."

Without a reply, I tightened the belt around my lap and sat back. I scanned the houses as we passed, but I saw nothing strange. Apparently, he didn't either. We never stopped.

The office was quiet as we entered. Jancey's assistant sat at her desk, but she had the phone to her ear as I hobbled into my office. I just hoped I didn't have to stay here all day. But I had the case files with me, so I thought I would revisit those.

Two hours later, Jancey stepped into the room. I couldn't read his facial expressions, which sent a shiver up my spine. "It's over. They're on their way here now. Felipe is en route to the emergency room. Maria and four other girls are safe. Blaine and his team are escorting them here."

I was so delighted at the news that the tears came without warning. "Thanks, Jancey, for everything."

With tear streaks down my face, I didn't want Blaine to see me like that. So I took a trip to the powder room. I stood at the coffee pot when Blaine stepped off the elevator in their full tactical dress. It stopped my heart to see him like this. Then Carter and Hudson followed, dressed the same. They were a force, no doubt.

Blaine's eyes met mine and rushed over to me. "Celeste. It's over."

"I know. Jancey told me. Now, I want to hear all about it." Then I looked over and saw four scared girls staring at me. "Come on. Let's take care of them first."

I went to them, introducing myself. They spoke English better than I expected. Maria was beautiful, with intense eyes. She studied everything around her. When I explained her parents were there, she said, "where?"

Then the elevator dinged, and when the doors opened, Antonio and his family stood face to face with Maria. When the realization struck, they raced into each other's arms. The reunion was special. Everything I had hoped.

Blaine suggested everyone move to the conference room. We followed Antonio's group as they held onto Maria for fear of losing her again. With counseling, I prayed she'd be okay.

Several female officers waited in the room for us. Jancey summoned them to help with the girls. But first, they need to know where their families live so they can be reunited.

Once things settled, Blaine took me into my office and closed the door. Then, he said, "are you ready to hear about the raid, or are you so happy with the outcome, that it doesn't matter?"

"The only part I'd like to hear is about Felipe. Did he confess or try to escape?"

"Fifty people swarmed his house at 3:00 am. Felipe's bodyguards were no match for our group. We subdued his guards quickly, but Felipe took refuge in a closet. He didn't know he helped us when he did that because it gave us time to scour the house for the girls. They were in a windowless basement room. But they partitioned the room off like apartments. Every girl had their own room and bath. They shared a kitchen and a sitting room. Once we found them and got them safely out of the way, we returned and handled Felipe. He suffered a broken arm, and a bullet wound to his foot."

"So, he'll survive and be able to stand trial." Then I paused. "Blaine, did anyone search him for a cyanide pill?"

He reached into his pocket, bringing out a small canister. "It was on his nightstand. I guess they never get too far away from it."

"The crime scene folks are there now. I've instructed Theo on what exactly we're looking for,

267

and he promised to call as soon as he finished. I'm going to the locker room to change. Then we're going home."

It was such a relief seeing him. Antonio popped into my office. "Celeste, I'll never be able to thank you for what you did for us. We're staying in the states, and I wanted you to hear it from me."

"That's fabulous, Antonio. You'll do good no matter where you live."

After I packed my things, Carter and Hudson stopped in. Carter said, "Take care, Celeste. I'm sure we'll be seeing you."

"Thanks, guys, for watching over me."

Blaine stood outside the door as I spoke with his unit. I wouldn't have survived without them. Then we all traveled to the safe house, packed our things, and headed out in different directions. Blaine drove me to his house. I was uneasy at first, but he calmed me.

His house was a modest ranch style, with siding and stone. He kept the yard manicured, and the driveway swept. Blaine entered the two-car garage and parked, leaving an available one next to his. He carried our bags as I maneuvered around the car into the kitchen.

The kitchen had a remodeled look to it. It boasted stainless appliances, a flat-top stove, and a massive vent over the stove. "This is gorgeous, Blaine. Are you the designer?"

"I'm glad you like it. When I bought it five years ago, I worked with a construction crew to remodel some portions of the home. Here, I'll set you up in the bedroom on this side of the house. It has a bath, too."

I nodded because the gesture was the sweetest. After he had placed my bags on the bed, he showed me the rest of the house. It equally impressed me. After lunch, he laid down for a nap, and I moved to the backyard.

There was a deck with only two steps to the ground, chairs, and an umbrella. I plopped down in the sunshine on a chaise, intending to finish my book. That didn't happen. Instead, I dozed.

Blaine woke me later in the afternoon, and he joined me on the chaise beside me. "I just got off the phone with Theo. We have enough evidence between what he found at Felipe's house and the workers to convict Felipe, his nephews, and the shooters."

"Oh, Blaine. That's fantastic. I feel like an immense weight lifted from my shoulders. There's no way I can repay you and your team for what you did for me."

Blaine nodded, "I've been thinking about that." He paused as he watched my head tilt. "I want you to stay here with me. You have your own room and bath. We'll share a kitchen and a family room. There's still so much that you must handle with the job change and the move. You need not worry about a place to stay. Think about it. You don't have to answer right now."

"I will. Thanks for the offer."

The rest of the day flew past with me on the phone, arranging for the move. Blaine drove me to my follow-up appointment a day early because I needed to be in Colorado Springs for my Realtor.

Blaine went with me to see the doctor. It pleased the doctor to see my progress. He asked me to stand with the weight on my leg. Once I stood, he asked me to walk into the room. I did. Then he watched me walk around the office. While I felt a twinge, he said that was normal.

I left the doctor's office, holding my crutches. He suggested I keep them in case anything happens.

It felt so good using both legs to walk to the car. That night, Blaine took me out to dinner to celebrate. Then we crashed early. We had a lot of sleep to make up.

The following day, the front page of the newspaper said it all. The headline read, "Busted!" Blaine, Carter, and Hudson had their photo taken as they stood behind the captain, ATF and FBI during a press coverage.

Blaine walked into the kitchen, and when I looked up, he rubbed his eyes. "Good morning." I offered.

"Good morning." He muttered. Once he poured coffee, he sat beside me at the table. Then smiled and asked, "Have I told you how happy I am that you're here?"

Books by Series

Books by Series Continued

Detective Clint Rugbee

Murder at Beachside Book 1

Waves of Murder Book 2

About the author:

A.M. Holloway is an author of murder, mystery, crime, and suspense books with a dash of romance for added excitement. She was born and raised in Georgia and still lives in the northwest part of the state. When not writing, you will find her with family enjoying the outdoors or sitting in her favorite chair daydreaming about her next book.

Visit **www.amholloway.com** for new releases and to sign up for my reader's list or simply scan the code.

Also follow me on:

Facebook @amhollowaybooks

Instagram @amhollowaybooks

Made in the USA
Middletown, DE
22 October 2023